From
Hell
2
Heaven

◦◦◦≪≫◦◦◦

THROUGH THE EYES OF A P.I.

BILL PERRY

ISBN 978-1-0980-6345-0 (paperback)
ISBN 978-1-0980-6346-7 (digital)

Christian Faith Publishing, Inc.
832 Park Avenue
Meadville, PA 16335
www.christianfaithpublishing.com

Editor: Jonathan Hamilton

Printed in the United States of America

I want to first give thanks to GOD for giving me the vision to write this book.

My Wife Dorla Perry

Thanks to my wife Dorla for her continued support and being the Prayer Warrior that she is.

Mr. Percy & Mrs. Irene Perry, where my book dream came about

To my mom and dad, Mrs. Irene & Mr. Percy Perry for being the best parents ever and for the gamble with my moms life to give me life with my dads support.

I want to also thank Bishop Rick Thomas and Pastor Al Scavon for seeing the vision and advising me to follow it.

I want to thank Private Investigator Wayne Weatherford & Maryann Chavous for their undying support.

I also want to thank Anthony Alford for seeing my vision even though he is blind. (blind faith if you will)

I also want to give thanks & a Salute to all of the countless Veterans that gave their time to talk with me.

I would like to Thank Marty Ruane for your service & sacrifice for our country & also from a personal point of view, you our friend are an incredible individual.

I would also like to give a thank you to Vinny Parco for signing me up to get my Private Investigations license & giving me the knowledge, experience & support that I have in P.I. work.

Juan Montalvo for his support with our websites & being a Awesome friend putting up with my computer knowledge (which is none).

Also, thanks to Art & Cheryl Tillberg for their support.

Eric Salna Meterologist & his wife Jane for their support on the book as well as other projects.

Theme Song Writer Ramon Robinson (Absoloot).
I Want To Be An American Soldier

Another huge thanks to Ramon Absoloot Robinson for the theme song for the book (I want to Be An American Soldier) as well as his support.

Also, Carl & Brizi Robinson for their support.

A huge thanks to Karen Moreau for always taking & answering our office calls even though she is going through some really difficult times.

Also, Keisha Bell for her support.

I want to thank Sid Kramer for always showing up & giving your support.

A big thank you to Private Investigator Jeffrey Taylor for always answering my calls.

Private Investigator Lydia Jones thanks for your support.

I want to thank Hy Hearst for his Legal advise as well as being my biggest critic.(all taken with Love)

Also thank you to Jasmin Redden for her relentless work ethic on multiple projects.

We would like to give thanks to Rachel Tourgeman & the Powerhouse Members with Florida National University for their continued effort to eliminate the unthinkable Human Trafficking. You always gave us the mic to spread the word concerning our projects & for that we thank you. We also want to congratulate you on your new Live Facebook & You Tube Show entitled: On Point With Rachal Tourgeman.

Gone to Early & Never Forgotten R.I.P.

Also, I want to give thanks to Private Investigator Yana Dee Dushanova for her support and speaking as if from another dimension in her final days, prophesized that this book had to be delivered.

Darren Maharaj, you my friend will never be forgotten. Even though you were going through some difficult times, you always had encouraging words & for that I thank you.

Also, I would like to thank James Warrington not only for your support with the book but also for your service for our country in Vietnam.

Contents

Title: From Hell 2 Heaven—Through the Eyes of a PI
Main Character (Protagonist): Murdock Grey a.k.a. Cider (CIA Operative)
Main Character (Antagonist): Abraham
Supporting Characters:

- Nadia Grey—the wife of Murdock Grey
- Bobby and Janine Pierce—friends of Murdock
- Bill Perry—PI
- Ron and Joe—PIs on Bill's team
- Danika Legrassi and Jaiden Santos and Kai Day Dream Girls on Bill's team
- Kathy Morris—Nadia's best friend
- Adam Morris—Kathy's husband
- Anthony Alford—the blind PI and Wayne Weatherford—PI
- John Brooks—the husband of Sarah Brooks (Kids: Jess, 6, and Alex, 3)
- Black soldier named Showboat, part of Platoon 3—the comedic relief
- Chevelle MP of the female barracks—married to Narc Agent Ramon (Miami)
- Narc Agent Jake—partner of Ramon
- Luiz—a big-time drug dealer in Miami
- Leo—familiar with Ramon

Acknowledgments

A special Thanks to Bobby White for your support on this project. We Salute you Sir for the tireless hours through the VFW POST 8195 that you put in helping our Veterans who are dealing with Post Traumatic Stress Disorder. The before mentioned Man Marty is proof that the work that you do for our Veterans WORK. I quote "THAT MAN SAVED MY LIFE" I heard it from multiple Veterans & you deserve recognition for that. Thanks again for inviting myself & Wayne to Post 8195 to get the unbelievable stories straight from the Veterans who were there on the front lines to give us, The American People the Freedom we enjoy today. You Sir & all Veterans are truly the Heroes of America. God bless you & we pray for your continued service.

Chapter 1

A Long Way from Home

The sun was rising on a Friday summer morning in South Florida off the east coast. An alarm clock blared at 6:00 a.m. as the sunlight seeped through the bedroom window of CIA Operative Murdock Grey. Murdock reached over to the nightstand and felt around to silence the alarm. As he rolled over, he discovered his wife was awake and already out of bed. Murdock got out of bed, put on his robe, and made his way toward the kitchen. He could hear the sizzle of turkey bacon on the stove and a steaming coffeepot. The aroma of freshly brewed coffee and breakfast filled the air.

"My love, you in here?" Murdock called out as he made his way into the kitchen.

"Yes, babe," Nadia responded as she proceeded to pour coffee into her husband's favorite coffee mug. It's inscribed with the Bible verse of Psalm 121: "I will lift my eyes to the hills from whence cometh my help." That was his dad's favorite verse when Murdock was a young kid growing up. Nadia slid some eggs, turkey bacon, and toast unto her and Murdock's plates; they made their way to the dining area and took their seats. Murdock thumbed through the *USA Today* paper while sharing in small talk with his wife over breakfast.

"I have some great news to share, my love," said Nadia nervously but with excitement as she reached across the table and clutched Murdock by his forearm.

"What's going on, honey?" Murdock replied.

"I had my six-month checkup with Dr. Neuschafer, and well… we are three months pregnant."

Murdock dropped his newspaper on the table. "Really? That is the best news, my love."

Nadia replied, "Are you sure this is what you wanted?"

Murdock responded, "Without a doubt, you'll be the best mother in the world, Nadia. This was GOD's will!" They leaned toward each other and engaged in a kiss. Moments later, Murdock's cell phone chimed, indicating he just received an e-mail from the agency. He was being assigned to a detail in Afghanistan called Operation Abraham.

The e-mail read,

SUBJECT: RE: Operation Abraham

Greetings Mr. Grey,

The agency hopes this message finds you well. The intelligence community has been paying close attention to the activities of an internationally recognized terrorist known by the name Abraham. All of the intelligence collected thus far suggests that Abraham has firsthand knowledge of an extremely sensitive nature that potentially threatens the national security of America and our global allies. The main objective of "Operation Abraham" will be to acquire new intelligence concerning Abraham, his allies and to bring them into custody for questioning. You will be accompanied by several other members of the agency and of the armed forces for this mission. Our sources suggest that Abraham's last known whereabouts was a remote village in Afghanistan. Your team's deployment date has been set for Saturday June 01, 2019. You and your team will be received by Basaam Mikhail and Bashir

Ram, two local U.S. allies in the region. Further updates and details concerning your mission will be provided upon your arrival to the pre-determined rendezvous point in Afghanistan.

Regards,
Intelligence Community
Washington D.C.

Murdock closed his e-mail and placed his phone down on the table.

"Everything all right, love?" Nadia asked.

"I'm being deployed this Saturday to Afghanistan," Murdock replied as he held a blank stare out the sliding glass dining room windows. Nadia stood up and walked around the table behind Murdock. She wrapped her arms around his upper body in assurance that all would be well. Murdock's phone rang; it's his longtime friend and partner John Brooks.

"What's up, John!" Murdock answered the phone.

"Another day in paradise, bud!" John said. "You got the unwanted dinner invite too?"

Murdock chuckled and responded, "Yep, Nadia and I were just talking about it." John and Murdock went way back and not just during their years of public service but as young men growing up as well. John had been part of the agency for a number of years, nearly as long as Murdock.

"Just like old times. See ya soon, brother," said John.

"My thoughts exactly, man. Send my love to Sarah and the kids," Murdock replied as they hung up.

*****

John and his wife, Sarah, continued prepping their kids, Jess and Alex, for day care and school. John turned to put the milk back in the fridge and continued his discussion with Sarah. "Honey, you know I've been in the service for nearly ten years, and I always have faith that GOD will protect me. But this one feels different. It feels—"

Sarah interrupted, "But nothing, John. GOD has always protected and always will protect our family."

John nodded in agreement. Sarah leaned and gave John a quick kiss on the cheek as she helped him adjust his tie on her way out the door. Jess and Alex gave their dad a hug as they followed their mother outside.

"Love you, guys!" John shouted as he stood in the doorway watching Sarah and the kids reverse out of the driveway and continue down the street.

*****

Early Saturday morning, Nadia and Murdock headed to the Executive Airport in Broward County. The car ride was quiet as the two of them held on to each other's hand; the radio played low in the background. The Greys pulled into the airport and up to the hangar the same time as John pulled up in a taxicab. John exited the cab as Murdock and Nadia got out of their car.

"Looking pretty good for an old man!" John heckled at Murdock with a grin running across his face. The two men shook hands. "Nadia, you're looking beautiful as always," John continued.

"Too bad we can't say the same for you," Murdock retorted, and all three burst into laughter. Nadia popped the trunk so Murdock can grab his luggage. Murdock and Nadia hugged and kissed once more before Murdock walked her to the driver's side and opened the door for her to get inside.

"You and John better take good care of one another," said Nadia as she shifted the car into reverse.

"No worries, Nadia. Like the insurance company says, he's in good hands."

*****

First Battalion, Third Marines

Four months had passed since Murdock and the team were deployed to Afghanistan on Operation Abraham. Murdock and his team were deep in the heart of Afghanistan. Basaam and Bashir had proven themselves to be loyal allies to the team. They both assisted the team in following leads, collecting intelligence, and navigating the city. A local informant working for Bashir had an address on a potential safe house location where Abraham was held up.

"What percentage is Abraham likely to be there?" asked Special Agent William McCormick.

"Up to 65 percent chance based on what my people are telling me," Bashir replied. Up to this point, the info provided by Bashir and Basaam had been relatively accurate thus far, but McCormick was not totally convinced that Bashir and Basaam were to be totally trusted.

John turned to Murdock and said, "What'd ya think, brother? It's your call." Murdock sat and gazed at the map laid out by Bashir as he awaited a response from the WH. Murdock addressed the team, "The WH confirmed the data provided by Bashir and his people. We got the green light. We move in on the spot tomorrow, after sunset."

That night, John and Sarah were able to communicate via FaceTime video messages sent back and forth. John sent a video message to Sarah just before going to bed at 11:00 p.m. his time but 2:30 p.m. back in the United States. When Sarah received the notification of a new message from John, she called the kids over, saying, "Kids, come quickly. We have a new message from Dad!" Jess and Alex immediately abandoned the cartoon show they were watching and made a quick dash to sit with their mom on the couch to watch John's video message. When Sarah opened the attachment, the image of John came up on the iPad screen. Instant smiles gleamed across the face of the kids, overjoyed to see their father's image on screen.

Sitting in his small room, curtain dangling in the background, John started his video by greeting the family and telling Sarah how much he loved and appreciated her and that he could hardly wait to see her and the kids again. John shared as much as he could about his day and the day that was ahead of him. "Honey, I have to be honest with you. This Operation Abraham is unlike all the other details I've been assigned to in the past. It just feels different." John was summing up his message. At that point, Sarah detected a difference in John's demeanor, but she couldn't quite figure out exactly what the issue may have been. John ended his message asking for continued prayer and telling the family he loved them and looked forward to seeing them soon.

The next day, during the late evening time, the sun was starting to set; it appeared to be another typical day in the dry and hot Afghan desert. Murdock and his men were moving through the town of the surrounding villages. They were on track to the location where they suspected Abraham was being held up.

"Guys, I got the location in sight," said John.

"This just feels too easy," McCormick whispered to one of his comrades. Murdock ordered the team to close in on the location.

"We're about fifty yards from the location," John relayed to the team.

All of a sudden, a firefight erupted in the center of the local town square when a group of unidentified hostiles opened fire on

Murdock and his team. The town locals all scattered in any direction for cover. Murdock and the team ran for cover behind any structure that could protect them from the overwhelming assault of AK-47 bullets pouring in on their location. Debris, broken glass, wood particles, and desert sand flew into the air as bullets whistled through the air near Murdock and his men. They returned fire on the encroaching hostiles.

During the exchange, John was pinned down behind a stack of wooden crates. While returning fire, he was struck by a bullet and took a knee behind the crates. John cried out, "I've been hit!"

Murdock shouted back at John, "Stay down! Stay down! We're coming! Stay down!"

In that moment, John thought of Sarah and the kids. He was brought back to the memory of the front yard of his home, his wife sitting on their oak wood bench he made himself. The kids were playing in the sprinklers, and Sarah gazed lovingly into John's eyes.

On the other side of the world, back in America, Sarah was standing at the end of her yard at the mailbox holding a conversation with the neighbor, while the kids were playing with their new puppy. Suddenly, a feeling of anxiety and terror gripped Sarah. She said to the neighbor, "Something is wrong. Terribly wrong." In an attempt to console her, the neighbor reminded her how long John had been in the service and that he would return home safely just as he always did in the past. The neighbor reached out to pat her on the back; but Sarah pulled away, turned to her kids, grabbed them up, and started making a nearly mad dash to her front door. The neighbor tried to restrain her but to no avail. Sarah was in such a frantic mood she nearly ran into the front door as she turned and kicked the door close behind her.

Back in Afghanistan, the firefight continued between Murdock's team and their opponents. John was still pinned down by oncoming fire. So far, Murdock and the team had not been able to extract him from the point of attack. John was losing a tremendous amount of blood, and by this point, he could no longer muster the strength to return fire to defend himself. John turned and sat with his back to the attackers. John's hands began to tremble as his body went into medical shock due to the loss of so much blood. He grasped on to his dog tags; the rattling of his tags in his trembling hands played an ambient echo against the background noise of gunfire swirling in from the enemy. With every beat of his heart, John lost more blood. He was near the point of passing out; John could sense the end was nearing. He bowed his head in prayer, saying, "Lord, I don't exactly know what you have in mind for me. Please, please forgive me! Please save me!" And with that, John slowly drew his last few breaths, closed his eyes, leaned over against the wall, and died.

The enemy assault was diminished. The hostiles slowly began to retreat as Murdock and his men courageously fought for survival. From all directions, Murdock and his men closed in on John's location, only to find they were too late—John was already gone. One of his team-mates, a man equally as religious as John was, attested to the fact that he believed he could actually see the angel of death encroaching on the lifeless body of John as they approached, seemingly like a dark shadow spiraling around his space. He said the image retreated back into the shadows of the building as the team got closer to John's space. The team mourned the loss of their teammate in that moment. They covered his body and carried him away from the point of attack.

*****

Operation Abraham was not the only conflict currently playing out in the deserts of Afghanistan. In a remote area of Afghanistan, not far from ground zero of Operation Abraham, a group of American soldiers was assigned to the area. The group was identified as Platoon 3. Platoon 3 was in a hotbed of activity and surrounded by local hostiles with links to the Taliban and other known terrorist groups. One of the men in Platoon 3 went by the nickname Showboat. Cocky, young, and lacking experience in the field, his nickname described his nature perfectly—a whole lot of talk but not a whole lot of ability. One day, during a routine tour of the area, Showboat disrupted the silence of the platoon, blabbing on and on about what he would do if he came across the creeps. Showboat bragged to his group, saying, "Maan, let me near a sniper! I'm gonna cut his eyes out and sneak up on him like a ninja." He struck an awkward karate pose like a black Bruce Lee in his mind, turned to his comrade Frankie, and said, "Frankie, you know what I'd do? I'd cut him up!"

Frankie calmly replied, "I'd love to see that, Showboat."

Showboat continued his nonsensical rant as the group moved through the streets. Showboat was up front conducting his rant and didn't realize that his team had taken a detour from the route they were originally on. Showboat continued down the path and made a left turn at the corner of a building and right into a group of enemy snipers preparing for their next set of enemy targets. Showboat stopped cold in his track with his gun still in his hands and was nearly paralyzed with fear. He felt behind him to see if he can locate a nearby teammate but felt no one. At that moment, a cold chill ran up his spine as he came to the realization that he was all alone and facing down the enemy. The snipers locked eyes on him. Showboat screamed like a little girl, turned around, and ran in the opposite direction, screaming, "Oh lawd help me, JESUS!" The enemy was in hot pursuit of Showboat, right at his heel with knives and weapons.

Not so far of a distance, Showboat saw a wall and decided to try to scale over to safety. As he made the daring leap, his pants buckle came undone; and as he made his way over the wall, Showboat gave the enemy a show they were not expecting as the rear of his pants began to fall down. The entire time he was attempting to climb over, Showboat was screaming to his comrades, "Help me! Help me get over this wall!" The Taliban came to the realization they were outnumbered by the American soldiers and quickly retreated.

"Next time ya might not be as lucky. Stay in formation!" Frankie shouted as they hoisted Showboat over the wall from the clutches of their enemies.

The female barracks were also positioned in Afghanistan and headed by Sgt. Chevelle Diaz. Chevelle had been a member of the U.S. armed services for nearly ten years. Her husband, Ramon Diaz, was a fifteen-year veteran narcotics detective. The other night, while Chevelle and Ramon were catching up with each other via video call, Ramon mentioned the fact that he and his partner would be conducting a special sting operation related to a case they were working on for the past several weeks. The next day, during a casual conversation with her longtime friend Jessica, Chevelle opened up about her husband's line of work back home in Miami, Florida. As Chevelle recalled this conversation with her teammate, worry took hold of her. Jessica can sense Chevelle's nerves and tension and asked her, "Why are you worried?"

Chevelle replied, "He sounded different over the phone last night, not himself at all."

Meanwhile, in Miami, Florida, Ramon and his longtime partner Jake were preparing to move in for the bust on the case they'd been working for weeks. They hopped in a dark-green classic 1975 Ford Mustang Shelby with white racing strips running down the middle and headed to the predetermined location for the drop. On the ride over, Ramon started telling Jake how much he can't wait for this detail to be over and how much he enjoyed working with Jake over the years. Jake can sense that Ramon was being overly sentimental. Jake turned to Ramon and said, "What the heck are you talking about? It's no different than any of the other hundreds of jobs we've done. No different!"

Ramon reached over to give Jake a one-armed hug, and Jake shrugged and shoved Ramon's arm away. Jake told Ramon, "What are you doing? Don't be putting no bad luck on me, man!"

Once they pulled up to the Black Bay Warehouse, they radioed for backup to take their designated positions as they moved in to make the drop. Ramon and Jake took a deep breath and prepared themselves mentally for what they must do. Steady on the outside, there was nervousness on the inside, fear of the unknown, and uncertainty about their futures. When they walked into the warehouse, Ramon noticed two men of similar height standing near a table holding a conversation. One of the two gentlemen, named Luiz, left the table and walked toward Ramon and said, "I got the goods. You got the money?"

Jake responded, "We've got the money right here." Jake patted the black duffel bag he's carrying. All of a sudden, another man by the name of Leo walked into the room. Ramon caught a glance of his face and recognized him from somewhere. Ramon quickly turned his face as he did not want Leo to notice him. Leo approached Luiz and asked, "Do you know these guys?"

"Aren't they Joe's guys?" Luiz replied. There was a moment of dead silence. Leo took one glance at Ramon and recalled where he last saw him. It was in the middle of the day on a Saturday in downtown Miami near the Wynwood area. Leo was being escorted out of a five-star hotel by one of his bodyguards. As Leo approached the back passenger side of his black Cadillac Escalade, he caught a glimpse of Ramon and his partner Jake stepping out of a small café across from the hotel. Leo noticed that both Jake and Ramon were wearing detective badges around their neck.

Leo turned to Luiz, broke the silence, and said, "No, they aren't Joe's guys. They're lousy cops!" Luiz instantly reached for his Glock 19, took aim, and fired at Ramon and Jake, who both instinctively took cover, pulled their Berettas, and returned fire. Suddenly the room erupted with the sound of gunshots followed by the chimes of brass shell casings bouncing across the cold warehouse floor. As Ramon maneuvered to take cover from the assault of gunfire, a round from Leo's Desert Eagle punctured Ramon's bulletproof vest, pierced him in his left lung, and spun him around as he fell to the floor.

"Ramon!" Jake shouted as he burst into a sprint toward his fallen comrade. As Jake made his way toward Ramon, he returned fire. One of his shots partially found its intended target, grazing Leo across the right side of his neck. Luiz proceeded to help a now-wounded Leo toward the rear of the warehouse to make their escape before cops swarmed the place. Jake reached Ramon and turned him over to assess the damage. He grasped Ramon's right hand.

"No, no, no, my GOD! She's coming home soon!" said Jake as he shook Ramon in an attempt to prevent him from losing consciousness. Ramon looked up to Jake and started to reminisce of times past with his wife. Early on a Sunday morning, the sun rose, shining through the eastern slide glass windows of Ramon and Chevelle's waterfront condo overlooking the sandy shores of Miami Beach. The shadow of Chevelle's silhouette danced across the kitchen floor as she moved back and forth from countertop to stove. Her long brown hair was pulled back in a bun. She was wearing only her black lace underwear and a white tank top embroidered by her university alumni logo. Ramon exited the bedroom, wearing his bathrobe. Upon entering the kitchen, he came up behind Chevelle and wrapped his arms around her waist and placed a gentle kiss on the back of her neck. He leaned toward her left and whispered into her ear, "I love you, Chevy."

She turned around. They gazed into each other's eyes and shared a kiss. Chevelle embraced Ramon and said, "I love you too." She turned, picked up their plates, and headed toward the balcony patio. Ramon was standing in the kitchen watching her from behind as she pushed the sliding glass door open with her left foot. Chevelle glanced back over her shoulder and said to Ramon, "Stay with me. Stay with me."

The image of Ramon's wife became dim and shallow; her voice turned to a faint echo in the distance. Ramon slowly regained consciousness, his eyes fluttering open to see his comrade Jake hovering in his face shouting, "Stay with me! Stay with me!" Jake heard the team moving in. He shouted out, "Officer down! Officer down! Over here!" Ramon's breathing became shallow. He's panting with quick short gasps for oxygen. He looked up to Jake now with tears filling up his eyes and whispered, "Brother, please tell Chevy I'm sorry and that I love her."

Jake responded, "You can tell her yourself. We're not losing you today!"

Ramon started coughing up blood. Suddenly a sense of an eerie, unknown, unseen dark shadow spiraling vaguely was near and faded away quickly. His presence can be felt but not touched. The sound of his movement in the warehouse whistled past the place where Ramon was lying in a gust of wind. He was a figure formed only by the dark shadow of the night skies. Ramon can now feel its very presence enveloping the place where his body lay. Ramon's panting for air got slower, and his grip grew weaker. He took three big gasps for air. On the final and third gasp, his hand went limp inside Jake's hand. His eyes were still open, but he was gone. Jake reached up and gently closed the eyes of his fallen teammate and friend, bowed his head, and subtly wept in silence.

Blessed to be Home Safe, some are not so lucky

Police and EMTs stormed in, stepping over the bloody mess, arriving just seconds after Ramon passed away. Medics attended to Jake and began performing CPR on Ramon. Hurrying him to the back of the ambulance, Ramon was rushed to Johnson Memorial Hospital. Despite all fire rescue efforts, Ramon was pronounced dead on arrival to Johnson Memorial. The field sergeant made arrangements to notify Ramon's wife, Chevelle, and immediate family members.

The news of her husband's death was channeled through a series of messages and finally reached Chevelle's base stationed in Afghanistan. Jessica intercepted the news once it reached base and took it upon herself to relay the heartbreaking news to Chevelle. Jessica was an eight-year servicewoman and had been in this situation before, but never was it this close to home; never was it her best friend whom she had to face to deliver this sort of news. Jessica made her way across the compound toward Chevelle's quarters. Chevelle was completing a debriefing with her team concerning new information received from the intelligence community. Jessica greeted Chevelle. The weight of the burden on her heart could be seen clear as day in her face.

"Is everything okay? You look worried," said Chevelle.

Jessica responded, "Can I speak with you for a moment in private please?" When they had stepped outside behind the station, Jessica began to break the news. "What I have to tell you is not going to be easy to hear or accept, and I wish it could be someone else telling you this but—"

"Jess!" Chevelle interrupted. "What is it? What happened?"

"It's Ramon. We just got word that something went terribly wrong during the sting operation in Miami. I'm sorry, Chevy, but we've been told that he didn't make it." Instantly, Chevelle's complexion became pale; a blank stare ran across her face as she attempted to comprehend what she had just been told. Chevelle sat on the water cooler by the station, buried her face into her cupped hands, and began sobbing over the loss of her best friend, her partner and husband. Jessica sat and wrapped her arms around her in an attempt to console her through it all, but she was overcome with grief and sorrow.

Back at ground zero for Operation Abraham, Murdock and his men surveyed the aftermath of the ambush and continued to press on pushing the enemy further into retreat. During the intense and bloody firefight, the team lost John. John was a big contributor to the success of Murdock's team from a strategy standpoint, but now he's gone.

"Damn it!" exclaimed McCormick. He was upset by the loss of John, a man he considered his mentor. The sight of John's lifeless body lying in the wreckage and debris sent McCormick off the rails. Will McCormick was the youngest member of Murdock's unit and may lack temperament at times, yet he's definitely no less qualified than the other special agents in the group. "Those no-good bastards! I want their heads!" shouted McCormick as he turned over the remains of a broken wooden table.

Murdock swiftly moved in and grabbed McCormick and threw him against the wall, pressing his forearm across his neck. "Get ahold of yourself! Do you want to die out here too? You're making yourself an easy target for an enemy that is still out there!"

"Sir, we got those towel heads on their heels. Can we just get in there and do our jobs?" said McCormick. Murdock released him from the wall and stared him down. "We have a very narrow window of time to finish our counterstrike. Whatever we're going to do, we need to do it now."

Murdock responded, "I know."

McCormick did not know how to read the poised demeanor of his unit leader. "That's it? That's all you have to say? We are getting battered out here, and all you have to say is I know!"

Murdock's expression changed, beyond annoyed with Will at this point. "William, I know exactly what I'm doing. Now I'm going to ask you one time and one time only to shut the hell up!" Murdock shouted as he stepped into Will's face. "Are we clear?" Murdock continued.

"Yes, sir, we're clear," said McCormick while still maintaining a look of defiance across his face.

Murdock's team continued to advance their counterstrike in what had become a nearly two-hour firefight. Approaching what appeared to be the building serving as the hub for the enemy, Murdock's men quickly moved up the two-story structure and directly up to the door behind which they suspected was the enemy. On the other side of the door were bare walls, a pantry door leading to another part of the building, and a single wooden chair occupied only by an Afghan woman dressed in all black. Her only apparent company were two young children holding on to her legs. The Afghan woman sat with perfect posture, her head erect, her hands resting on her lap with her palms face down. She was draped in her ethnic black robe, which covered her from head to toe. A hint of sadness laced her eyes as her attention was drawn to the patter of heavy footsteps approaching her front door.

Murdock signaled each of his teammates into position. He proceeded to kick in the door. McCormick was the first one through the door. Instantaneously, one of the two little children leaped to his feet and ran toward the door. When McCormick caught sight of the little child running toward him, it caused him to hesitate for a fraction of a second. Suddenly one of the terrorist emerged from behind the pantry door, raised a black .45-caliber gun, and fired at McCormick. The moonlight gleamed off the chamber of the enemy's gun; a round exited the barrel, and a brass shell casing fell to the ground. The round pierced the front of McCormick's neck and exited through the back. McCormick shouted in pain and fell with his back against the brick wall into a sitting position. He clasped his hand over the hole in his neck. Blood was seeping through his fingers and running down his shirt.

"Cover me!" Murdock shouted as he went in to pull McCormick out of harm's way. The shots continued. The Taliban still had the woman and her two young kids hostage.

McCormick was having a difficult time breathing; blood was pooling up in his airway and lungs. "JESUS!" yelled McCormick as he coughed up blood.

"Hang in there, pal! Just hang on!" shouted Murdock as he applied pressure to the wound in William's neck. It appeared as though the death angel had returned to visit this team yet again. The presence of this shadow thief, the angel of death, stalked the gun smoke-filled air, his footsteps heard with the drop of every brass shell casing that hit the floor. Closer and closer he got with every blood-filled breath that McCormick drew. "Lord, please not now, not today," prayed McCormick. Tears formed in his eyes as he continued, "I-I'm so sorry. P-Please forgive me! Please save me!" He rolled his eyes up to look at Murdock.

"Oh no, you don't! Will, you can't, man!" Murdock's voice slightly trembled. He cleared his throat. "You still owe me fifty bucks, bro!" He laughed, causing McCormick to laugh, all while still choking on his own blood. "What about helping me finish all the new deck work I started in the backyard, huh? Who else is gonna hide with me in the garage with a six-pack while our ol' ladies stand up in the kitchen gossiping?" said Murdock.

"Pray, p-please pray," uttered a now-shivering McCormick. At this request, a tear rolled down the side of McCormick's dust-covered battered face. In a trembling voice, Murdock began to pray. "The Lord is my shepherd…" He was stammering. "I-I don't know what else to say, Lord… Please help."

A choked-up Murdock continued, "We have been walking through all of the valleys of death, but I will fear no evil." The thought of losing another friend gripped Murdock with emotion. He can't continue the prayer. William slipped out of consciousness. Murdock checked his pulse and started shaking him to try to revive him.

William was standing at the altar and can now see his young bride, Lorie, clear as ever; and a flashback took him on their wedding day, when she was walking toward him down the aisle. She was adorned by a splendid all-white dress and veil as their family and friends stood in agreement and celebration. William can see Lorie in the delivery room. Standing by her bedside, he gripped her hand in his as she gave one final push. The first cry of their newborn son fell on his ears, and tears of joy fell from William's and his wife's eyes as they both embraced their new son. Will entered the CIA HQ on his first day in the agency and was now being introduced to Murdock for the first time. They both shook hands, and Murdock motioned with his head and said to William, "Follow me," as they headed toward the briefing room. The memory reel continued to run across William's mind as Murdock desperately attempted to revive him. William and Murdock were standing around chatting near a charcoal-lit grill while the smell of fresh burgers and ribs filled the air. Meanwhile, their wives were monitoring the kids on the playground as their dogs played together in the grassy field.

The dust had not settled as the firefight between the Taliban soldiers and Murdock's men continued. Shell casings ricocheted off the wall next to Murdock and William. William stopped breathing and slowly slipped off into the embrace of death. Murdock immediately started administering CPR. After two or three cycles of CPR, he placed two fingers on the side of William neck and realized he no longer had a pulse. Murdock slid himself from underneath McCormick's limp body and gently placed his head down on the floor.

"Man down! I need a medic!" shouted Murdock over the radio. Gazing down at his fallen comrade, the steady chord of composure that Murdock had maintained suddenly snapped. Overcome with grief and emotion, the sorrow Murdock felt turned into rage. He stormed past his men in the doorway, drew his .45-caliber gun, took aim, and shot the Taliban soldier responsible for the death of McCormick. Two other Taliban soldiers crept up the stairwell on the opposite side of where Murdock and his men made entry. Murdock can hear the enemy footsteps approaching. Forgetting that he even had backup, he spun around, overlooking his left shoulder. He knelt, took aim, and shot the second and third Taliban soldiers. The first Taliban member was struck in the head, but Murdock struck the second soldier in the chest as they both tumbled backward, falling down the stairs one on top of the other. Murdock slowly walked down the stairwell where the two soldiers had fallen.

The soldier who was struck in the chest was still showing signs of life. Murdock proceeded to pick up a nearby steel rod and began beating the terrorist in the face. The blood splattered across Murdock's face as he smashed the enemy's skull and killed him there in the stairwell. Murdock came back up toward the top of the stairway and entered the main room again. As Murdock's men were tending to the hostages, the Taliban soldier who was responsible for McCormick's death began to stir.

"I got him, I got him," the Taliban soldier taunted Murdock in his broken English and had a sinister grin across his face. The taunts of the enemy reignited Murdock's fury. He walked over to the taunting soldier, picked him up over his head, and threw him down the stairs. As the soldier went tumbling down the stairwell, the back of his head bounced off one of the steps, killing him instantly. Murdock was going to continue after him to make sure he was dead; but his men, recognizing their leader had lost all composure, attempted to restrain him.

"It's over, sir, we've got the rest. Let's get outta here," said one of Murdock's men.

"Yeah, Murdock, they're all dead. Please, come on," said another soldier rather nervously. Murdock began to come back to his senses and was ushered away from the lifeless bodies of their enemies. The perimeter team scouted the building from top floor to bottom, but there was no sign of Abraham anywhere.

The sunrise of the next day shone light on the dark and brutal carnage that Murdock and his team were a part of the night before. Part of the team kept watch on the perimeter, and another part took time to assist in patching up their comrades as they awaited extraction. Suddenly a very familiar sound could be heard in the distance as two UH-60 Black Hawk helicopters approached the area where Murdock and his men were pinned down during the intense firefight with the enemy. The wind and dust kicked up into the air as the two U.S. choppers landed in the open desert area at the predetermined extraction point for Murdock and his team. After a nearly twelve-hour gun battle with the Taliban, Murdock and his men were bruised and battered, but all the more thankful to be alive. As the choppers landed, U.S. medics quickly hopped down to the ground with gurneys in hand. They made a generally fast assessment of the group and ran to those who appeared to be in worst physical condition in comparison to the others.

"Man, are we happy to see you, guys!" said one of the soldiers, Tommy, as he pressed a bloodstained rag up to the side of his dusty and bloody head. Medics hurriedly placed Tommy on a gurney and began tending to his wounds. While the medics prepped Tommy for the chopper, he noticed a symmetrical light moving across the ground where he lay.

"Hey, check this out," said Tommy as he pointed out the light to the medic who was patching him up. All of a sudden, a near-deafening sound rang the ears of all those standing nearby and literally shook the ground beneath their feet.

"Did you guys hear that? It felt like the earth was shaking!" shouted one of the wounded soldiers.

"Did you all see that? Seemed like a flash of lightning in broad daylight! It lit up the sky like it was night," said one of the medics.

The men now began whispering to one another as the paranoia of looming trouble crept into the mind of the group. The men assigned to the perimeter lookout started scouting for any potential sniper activity or enemy advancement.

"Impossible! There isn't a cloud in the sky," said Charlie, one of the field medics. Charlie continued, "What's that over there? I see some movement on that two-story building to the northeast of us." One of the perimeter lookouts used his long rifle scope to inspect the rooftop pointed out by Charlie. He can see what appeared to be a white cloth-like fabric, perhaps even a sleeve. But the soldier was unable to clearly make out what he was seeing because light coming from it was so bright, so he dismissed it, wondering what was it that was causing a glare due to the positioning of the building.

Murdock advised his perimeter team to remain on high alert until the med evacuation was completed. One by one, the team was prepped for export. Other soldiers on the team with prior medical experience also pitched in to help speed up the process. The last remaining members were all prepped and loaded unto the choppers. Murdock was the last to step foot off the field until all of his men had been prepped for takeoff. Murdock sat at the edge of his chair on the chopper, overlooking the area where he and his men fought for their lives a few hours ago. The faces of his fallen comrades, John Brooks and Will McCormick, flashed before his mind. He can still hear their voices echoing their last words before drawing their final breath. Murdock was saddened by the loss of John and Will, yet still grateful for his life and the lives of all those who survived. The place where the battle took place quickly became indistinguishable from the rest of the land below as the choppers moved swiftly toward a U.S. medical base. Murdock reached down and placed his hand on Tommy's shoulder as he lay on the floor with an IV in his arm and said, "We get to go home, brother, thank GOD. We get to go home."

Chapter 2

Welcome Home

Approximately six hours removed from a fierce gun battle with the Taliban, the evacuation choppers carrying Murdock and his team were approaching the U.S. medical base stationed in Landstuhl, Germany. Murdock raised his head, leaned toward the passenger window, and gazed down at the hospital facility. For the first time in what seemed like an eternity, Murdock caught a glimpse of the American flag flying high above the facility. The sight of Old Glory was a sober reminder a place approximating hell was a little bit farther behind him.

The chopper landed on the rooftop of the facility. Medical professionals quickly rushed Murdock in for X-rays, cleanup, and stitching. Dr. Ryan entered Murdock's room with X-ray sheets in hand.

"So what's the verdict, Doc? Safe to say I'm not pregnant," Murdock joked with a slight grin. The two men laughed.

"No, Murdock, you're not with child, but your test results reveal that you suffered some spinal damage," Dr. Ryan responded as he held the X-ray sheet up to the light. The MDs in Germany forwarded Murdock's profile to Florida. Murdock was prepped and airlifted to a top Florida medical facility for emergency surgery. During the fifteen-hour flight from Germany to the United States, Murdock had plenty of time to reflect on the hellish encounter with the Taliban and the brave men he fought beside who did not survive. Murdock dozed off during the flight and slipped into a nightmare. He was back in on the battlefields of Afghan territory. He can see his former comrades William and John off in the distance, but the enemy was pressing in on their location.

"Murdock! Help us please!" shouted John.

"I'm coming, guys!" When Murdock closed in on John and William's location, they were already dead, but Murdock knelt beside their bodies. Suddenly William grabbed hold of Murdock's arm with tears of blood streaming down his face and shrieked, "You let us die!" Murdock was jolted awake by the dream.

"You okay, sir?" asked one of the medics.

"Yeah, I'm fine. Just had a dream."

After landing at the airport, Murdock was assisted into a black SUV and transported to a Florida medical facility for surgery. Nurses received and prepped Murdock for surgery and began rolling him down the hallway to the operating room.

"Hey, Murdock! Small world, huh?" shouted Tommy as Murdock rolled by his bed, heading toward the operating room.

"We gotta stop meeting like this," Murdock jokingly said to Tommy. Upon entering the operating room, the primary surgeon came over to Murdock's bedside and assured him he will be as good as new when it was all finished. Dr. Delgado was a leading medical surgeon in South Florida with well over twenty-five-plus years of experience in the field of surgery and medicine. "This will be over before you know it," Dr. Delgado said to Murdock.

"That sounds good to me, but who's serving the cocktail?" Murdock asked, jokingly referring to the anesthesiologist. Suddenly the room began to fade as Murdock was being placed under anesthesia.

A few hours removed from his surgery, Murdock had been transferred to recovery and was slowly regaining consciousness. The door to Murdock's room slowly opened; and in came his wife, Nadia, and stood along his bedside. Nadia was now noticeably pregnant; her belly restricted her from leaning over comfortably to give Murdock a kiss. "My blessing in disguise... I'll take it," said Nadia as tears welled up in her eyes, and she caressed the side of Murdock's face.

"I missed you too, my love," Murdock said as he turned his head toward Nadia and smiled. The doctors cleared Murdock's surgery as an outpatient procedure and provided some take-home instructions and medicine for any pain he may experience. Nurses pushed Murdock out the main exit in a wheelchair as Nadia and her stepsister Kim pulled the car around front.

"Remember, no strenuous activities for a few days, Mr. Grey," said the nurse as he assisted Murdock into the car.

"Oh, believe me, he's in good hands. Thank you, guys!" Nadia responded.

It's a bright sunny day on the east coast of South Florida. The beaches were filled, restaurants were busy, and touring families were crossing the street left and right. Nadia approached a red light. There's almost an awkward silence despite talk radio filling the lull. You can tell that Nadia was searching for a topic to talk about as she ran her hand across the steering wheel. Her stepsister Kim was in the back, scrolling down social media on her cell phone. Murdock was simply enjoying the views of Highway A1A.

"Oh, so it's such a wonderful idea to write letters to the baby!" Nadia began. "Just so you know, I started a scrapbook with all the letters and pictures matched up." Nadia continued as she proceeded down South Beach.

"Do I get to see it, or is it a surprise after the baby is born?" Murdock was teasing his wife, because he knew she was not that good when it came to surprises.

A slight grin ran across Nadia's face. "Yes, I have to show you! I am super proud of it," Nadia replied.

"Great! That will prevent me from having to sneak a peek," Murdock jokingly said. In an excited reaction, Nadia grabbed Murdock by the arm. Murdock shouted and cringed in pain.

"Oh, babe! I am so sorry. I totally forgot about your wound. Are you okay?" Nadia said as she rubbed the back of Murdock's head.

Murdock had a quick flashback to the memory behind his wound, smiled, and said, "I'm fine. Just tired, is all."

They continued down South Beach. From the back seat, Kim spoke up. "Guys, we're passing through one of the hottest spots on the planet in Florida. South Beach!" Bicycle taxis passed by carrying a young couple down the strip as they sipped on their margaritas from coconut cups. On the other side of the street, you can see a group of young ladies in bikinis, with a drink in hand, heading toward the bar and a family of four sitting at a round table sharing laughs at the ice cream parlor.

Nadia pulled up to the front gates of their community. The security officer recognized Murdock from the passenger side. The officer waved and shouted, "Welcome home, Mr. Grey!" Murdock nodded and gave a quick wave back. As Murdock and the family made their way through the community, they can see there was a birthday party at the clubhouse for one of the residents. The pool area was packed out with kids playing, lounging parents, and guests. Nadia turned into their yard and parked in front of their two-car garage townhome. Though still a bit unsteady on his feet, Murdock exited the car first and made his way around to open the door for Nadia as Kim exited the back seat. One of the garage doors opened, and on the other side were family and friends with confetti and a large overhead welcome-home banner.

"Welcome home!" shouted the mixed crowed of family, coworkers, and friends. Murdock shook his head and chuckled in amazement at how many people showed up to his house to welcome him home. The crowd ushered him to the backyard, where there were tables and chairs set up, music playing, food, and a line of coolers across the lawn. Over on the grill was Murdock's longtime friend Ron Du-Pre. Ron raised a cup and shouted, "To our hero!" and the crowd repeated, "To our hero!"

Murdock turned, hugged, and thanked his wife. Then he slipped off into the crowd to greet and mingle with everyone else. As the evening progressed and Murdock was interacting with his people, Nadia noticed something in Murdock's demeanor that was different, almost strange; but she figured it was probably nothing to be worried about. The evening festivities began to die down; everyone who was invited started to leave. Murdock and Nadia shook hands and thanked everyone for coming. One by one they left until only Murdock and Nadia were at the house. Silence now replaced the music, laughter, chatter, and festivities.

Murdock sat outside alone on the back of his unfinished deck. He started to revisit the hellish nightmare he survived in the deserts of Afghanistan. He had a flashback, and suddenly the sound of gunshots started ringing throughout the backyard. Murdock can feel the shoulders of his fallen comrades pressed against him as they took cover from the oncoming fire from the enemy. He desperately tried to suppress the anxiety, stood up, shook his head, and walked off the deck.

Nadia came over, embraced him, and said, "Are you okay? You seemed like you were in a daze just now."

Murdock didn't know what to make of what he just experienced and did not want to cause his wife to worry. "I'm…uh…I'm fine. Just tired, I think," Murdock replied. Nadia asked him to go inside for bed. He took one final swig of the beer he had been holding, chucked it in the trash, and followed his wife upstairs to their bedroom.

Murdock and Nadia lay down in bed together. Nadia rested her head on Murdock's chest and started off their pillow talk. "I hope you enjoyed your party. We tried to make it special."

Holding her close and rubbing her shoulders, Murdock said, "My love, I appreciate what you all did. It was great." During their chat, the two of them fell asleep in each other's embrace. At some point during the middle of the night, a transformer blew out near Murdock's community. The explosion jolted Murdock awake; but not only did it wake him up, it also triggered flashback, an imaginative yet very real sense of danger inside him. In his mind, at this point, he was back in the deserts of Afghan land fighting for his life. The only things he can hear now were artillery, gunfire, and heavy machinery all around him. He ran downstairs and out the back door into the yard. The only visibility he had was coming from a flickering streetlight on the corner. Dazed and confused, Murdock was feeling around for his gun, a knife, or anything he can get his hands on to ward off the enemy.

Eventually, Nadia woke up when she realized Murdock had left the bed. She went downstairs and followed her husband to the backyard. "Mickey, baby, what's wrong? Why are you out here?" Nadia asked while standing in the doorway wearing just her nightgown.

The silhouette of his wife turned into the figure of a black-hooded terrorist intruder. Murdock was in full defense mode. He was ready to kill the figure before him.

Nadia started to approach her husband; but when she caught a glimpse of the rage in his eyes, she stopped cold in her tracks, paralyzed totally by fear. For the first time ever, Nadia found herself afraid of her own husband. "Mickey, baby, wake up. It's okay! You're home now." Nadia continued calling out. The terrorist figure now appeared to be surrendering, placing their hands in front of them. Nadia was an emotional wreck and crying. Nonetheless, she reached out to grab Murdock by the hand, not knowing if she was going to survive or not. "Wake up, my love, you're home."

Murdock gazed in her direction. The terrorist figure standing before him slowly began to transform into the familiar face of his wife. "Nadia?" he said, still dazed and confused.

"Yes, it's me," she replied.

"I could have…," Murdock hesitantly stammered. The realization that he may have only been seconds away from killing his own wife was too much for him to even say out loud. He could barely utter a word.

"It's all right. You were having a bad dream. Let's get inside, and we'll talk about everything in the morning."

*****

The next morning, the Greys woke up and headed downstairs to the dining area. It's a rainy and gloomy morning with a cloudy overcast. Murdock was sitting at the dining room table having breakfast. Nadia sat directly across from him. There's an awkward silence in the air. Nadia gave off a slight smile toward Murdock and started eating. Murdock took one more bite of food and placed his fork down. "Babe, I'm sorry if I scared you last night. Not sure what came over me."

Nadia reached across the table and rubbed the back of Murdock's hand. "It'll pass, Mickey. You're still adjusting to being back home and safe," she said. Nadia took another fork of food and put her head down in contemplation. "Mickey, what happened over there?" Nadia asked.

Murdock looked away from Nadia and out the window. "My love, we've been through this. It's classified information," Murdock said.

Nadia sighed and rolled her eyes. "Classified. You only use that word when you just don't want to talk about it."

She continued, "Look, it's not going to get any better if you bottle it all up inside. Don't push me out. I'm your wife. I love you, and I'm here to support you."

Murdock turned toward Nadia again, but before he can speak, she continued, "I want to help, but you have to let me in."

Murdock sat back in his chair and crossed his leg. "Sweetheart, you have enough to worry about right now, and besides, I've been assigned a counselor." After he finished, he took his wife by the hand and kissed it. "Now, where is that famous scrapbook you wanted me to see?" Murdock asked.

"Yay!" Nadia celebrated with excitement. Her hand still firmly in her husband's, she towed him down the hallway toward the last door on the right, which was the baby's room. The room was fully renovated and furnished a few weeks back. The room was filled with green décor, drapes, and more. In the right-hand corner of the room sat a white crib draped with green bedding. Murdock stood alongside the crib, ran his hands across the railing, and looked down, now imagining his newborn lying asleep in their crib.

Nadia headed over toward the window and reached into a box filled with all kinds of assortments, toys, and more. She pulled out the scrapbook and motioned for Murdock to go sit in the rocking chair off in the far left corner of the room opposite the crib.

"Have a seat, love," Nadia said as she made her way across the room with the scrapbook in hand. She took her seat on Murdock's lap. She opened the scrapbook containing all of Murdock's letters in chronological order that he wrote to home during his time in Afghanistan.

"Oh, baby, it's perfect. Thanks for working hard on this." Murdock pulled Nadia toward him and kissed her on the forehead.

"You really like it?" Nadia asked. "I just thought it'd be the perfect way for you to show your new son how much you loved him."

She continued, "I'm just so happy to have you home." Nadia's eyes started to well up with tears. "I was so worried about you, but now you're home for good," she said as she started kissing Murdock's face.

"Yes, I made it back home," Murdock said as he closed his eyes. He can see McCormick's face and remembered his death on the field. He sighed, rested his head against Nadia, and wrapped his arms around her as the scrapbook slid from her lap and unto the floor.

In the afternoon of that same day, Murdock was taking a nap in the living room on the couch when Nadia heard a knock at the door. She went to answer it, and she was pleasantly surprised to see it's one of Murdock's longtime friends named Bobby standing in the doorway with a big smile on his face.

"Nadia, my love," Bobby said as he opened his arms for a hug.

"Baby Murdock, my second love!" Nadia replied and hugged Bobby. "Mickey is taking an old-person nap on the couch in the living room. Come on in, and I'll grab you a drink."

Murdock woke up when he heard the front door close. "Honey, who's at the door?" he asked.

As Murdock was rolling over, Bobby ran into the middle of the living room and shouted, "Hey there, sexy thing!"

Murdock laughed at the sight of his buddy. "Keep your voice down. My wife may suspect something." Murdock joked with Bobby as he made room for him on the couch. Bobby came over and sat down on the couch next to Murdock. "So how ya been, Bobby?"

Bobby shrugged and said, "I'm good, bro." He went on to say, "Hey, some of the old crew is going out tonight for a few drinks, and they wanted you to come hang with us. You up to it?"

Murdock looked around the corner into the kitchen at Nadia. "I don't know, man. I don't really want Nadia going out in her condition right now."

Nadia made her way into the living room with two beers and a glass of iced tea on a tray. "Go on without me. I'll be busy working on the rest of the décor for the baby's room. Besides, you need to go hang with your boys and get a few drinks," said Nadia as she passed the beers to Bobby and Murdock.

"Deal. I'll come back for you tonight around ten!" Bobby shouted as he made his way out the front door.

Chapter 3

Scars and Stripes

Later that evening, Bobby came back to the Greys' house to pick up Murdock as planned. Murdock grabbed his jacket and headed over to Nadia who's sitting at the dining room table. "All right, babe, Bobby and I are heading out. Love you," Murdock said to Nadia as he leaned over to give her a kiss.

"Love you too, sweetie. Behave yourself tonight," Nadia replied as she walked them toward the front door. Murdock and Bobby hopped in his car, and they reversed out of the driveway. As they headed out of the community, Bobby started filling in Murdock on the plan for the evening. "So the guys have decided we'll meet at one of the bars on A1A road in Fort Lauderdale."

On a Friday evening, A1A was packed with stop-and-go traffic and people crossing the street. A line of exotic foreign cars stretched around the corner of one restaurant as the valet team hustled. Directly across the street, a group of beautiful young ladies in high heels and short dresses waited in line to get inside another lively nightclub. Murdock and Bobby were checked by security and granted entry to the bar. Once inside, straight ahead hanging above the bar was a banner that read, "Welcome Home, Cider!" Cider was Murdock's code name while in the service. The group cheered and applauded as Murdock made his way up to the concession of friends circling around the bar.

Bobby grabbed Murdock by his shoulders, came up beside him, and said, "Good to have you back home, buddy." Murdock grabbed a stool and sat at the bar. One of Murdock's friends, Brian, walked around to the front of the bar to greet Murdock with two shots of tequila in hand.

"Here's to the hometown hero!" Brian shouted as he passed a shot to Murdock.

"Bottoms up, pal!" Bobby shouted as everyone took their shots collectively.

Brian leaned over toward Murdock. "So be honest, big guy. How many of those young Afghani girls did you date while you were there?"

Bobby smacked Brian on the shoulder and said, "Seriously, man?"

Murdock took a swig of his beer and smirked. "None, Brian, I couldn't bear the thought of cheating on you," Murdock replied. The three men burst into laughter together. "Man, I had no time to fool around on Nadia. I was like a homesick puppy, writing letters back home all the time," Murdock continued.

"Nadia! Nadia! Where art thou, Nadia!" Bobby shouted, waving his arms in a dancing motion. The group erupted into laughter all at once. Bobby gestured to the bartender with money in hand and shouted, "One more round!" As the men carried on in their conversation, a group of very attractive young ladies noticed the group and started making their way toward the bar. One of the young ladies walked directly to Brian and started up a conversation. Another girl wrapped her arm around Brian's arm. "Come dance with us." Brian melted and instantly headed toward to dance floor. The other guys followed suit, except for Murdock.

"You guys go on. I'm not up for dancing right now," said Murdock as he took a swig from his beer bottle.

A young lady by the name of Maria walked over to Murdock and rested her hands and head on his shoulders. "Are you Cider?"

Murdock answered, "Yes."

Maria's eyes lit up with excitement. "What? The man of the hour does not dance. I think not."

Murdock gestured the group to go on without him to the dance floor. However, Maria decided to remain at the bar and take Bobby's now-vacant seat. Murdock's body language suggested he did not want to be bothered, but even so, he glanced in Maria's direction. And he thought to himself how he ended up sitting next to this curvy, 5'3" tall, 125-pound brunette wearing a fitted red dress and heels.

"I've heard so much about you. You're a real-life hero." Maria continued talking.

Murdock took a swig of beer. "I was just doing my job, but I'm still a marine."

Maria nodded in approval of what Murdock had just said. "I get it. I was in a war also," Maria said as she looked down into her half-empty glass.

"Where were you stationed? Afghanistan, Iraq?"

Maria shook her head. "No, not that kind of war. My-my ex-boyfriend." Maria began to stammer over her words, and tears welled up in her eyes as she continued to recall her past caught-up experiences in human trafficking relationship. "I've seen him do some terrible things, awful things, maybe even murder."

Across from Murdock and Maria, on the opposite side of the bar, sat Maria's now ex-boyfriend Hooker surrounded by his entourage. The bartender walked over to Hooker, who's now leaning against the bar glaring in the direction of Murdock and Maria.

"I got you another one, Hook. Just like you like it," said the bartender as he slid Hooker his drink.

Hooker pushed his dreadlocks to one side, reached into his top coat pocket, and pulled out a roll of money. The money was wrapped around a small baggie of cocaine. He peeled off a few bills and tipped the bartender. Ironically, one of the members of Hooker's entourage happened to be present at a narcotics raid. He peered at Murdock and Maria and nodded his head, indicating to them that they were on his radar.

"Yo, Hooker, that's ya girl with another mon. What type of mon are you? No respect, mon," said one of Hooker's cousins named Max as he smacked him on the shoulder.

Hooker gulped his shot of rum, slammed the cup down on the counter, and said, "The woman can't keep from being with a mon one night!" All of Hooker's buddies continued to chime in, echoing exactly the same message. Hooker's jealousy grew after every remark made by someone in his group.

"Breaks me heart, mon," said Hooker.

Maria rested her head on Murdock's shoulder. Murdock placed his arm around her in an attempt to console her. Hooker was staring from across the room and saw Murdock and Maria getting closer to each other.

Hooker's female companion latched on to his shoulder and said, "Hooker, baby. Don't pay her no attention. You got me now."

Hooker shrugged her off and shouted, "Shut up, okay, just shut up!" Hooker was now seething with anger and started cracking his knuckles. "I'm gonna go handle this myself," he said as he started making his way toward the bar where Murdock and Maria were sitting.

Murdock was holding Maria close to comfort her. Maria's internal battles were all too relatable to Murdock's own demons. Even he himself began to feel comfort in her embrace, but he started to feel guilty the instant his wife, Nadia, flashed across his mind. Maria moved in closer to Murdock to try to kiss him, but just before they did, Hooker and his people strode up.

"Yo, Maria, what the hell is going on here? Who ya friend?" Hooker asked Maria. Maria didn't even recognize him at first until he spoke. "Did I give you permission to be hanging and kissing over another man?" Hooker asked. Hooker's group started instigating and antagonizing the situation, egging Hooker on to be even more aggressive.

"You have no right to tell me who I can be around. We not even together anymore," Maria said to Hooker, with her hand still resting on Murdock's shoulder.

Hooker shook his head at Maria's comment. "Rights? I own you. You're mine until you're not anymore. Now let's go before you have to pay the price."

Murdock was starting to get edgy and interjected at this point. "Woah, relax, man. It's not what ya think."

Hooker responded to Murdock without even looking at him. "If I were you, hero, I'd mind my own business. This doesn't concern you."

Maria stood up. "Don't talk to him like that. He just got back from—"

Hooker grabbed Maria by the arm before she had time to finish her statement and snatched her toward the exit while shouting at her, "You're leaving with me now!"

Maria broke down and started crying as she said to Hooker, "All right, I'll go. Just please don't hurt him. He has nothing to do with this." As this commotion was taking place right before Murdock, a waitress popped a bottle of champagne open across the hall. Instantly Murdock froze in place and zoned out. He's experiencing a flashback of McCormick being shot. Murdock lost his sense of reality and slipped into a tunnel vision state of mind.

The club setting had now transformed into that old brick wall room where McCormick drew his last breath in Murdock's arms. Hooker was no longer a low-life thug in a bar but a bare-handed member of the Taliban advancing on Murdock. Murdock instinctively grabbed Hooker by the arm. Hooker turned and punched Murdock in the face. Hooker's entourage closed in on the area where Hooker and Murdock were now in a physical altercation. Murdock was momentarily dazed by the blow Hooker landed. He could hear the voice of John Brooks calling out, "Help! I'm hit!"

Hooker noticed Murdock was in a daze and tried to kick him in the head. Murdock spun out of the way and tripped Hooker with a sweeping reverse leg kick. Murdock got back to his feet. Hooker stood and charged at him and tried to tackle him. Murdock stopped his takedown attempt by putting him in a front headlock. He proceeded to land three hard knee strikes to his rib cage and midsection, ending with an elbow to the back of Hooker's head. As Hooker fell down to the ground on his hands and knees after the elbow blow to the back of his head, Max, Hooker's cousin, ran up behind Murdock and attempted to stab him with a knife. Murdock caught the reflection of Max in the mirror behind the bar. Just as Max raised his arm to stab Murdock in his back, Murdock spun around and grabbed Max by the arm. Murdock elbowed him in the face, breaking his nose; hip tossed him to the ground; and proceeded to break his arm. Max was now on his back screaming in pain. He looked down and saw his forearm bone was sticking out of his flesh.

Another one of Hooker's people tried to go after Murdock, but Bobby hip tossed him to the ground and drove his foot into his chest. "Don't even think about it," Bobby said. Murdock seriously injured several other members of Hooker's group by the time Hooker regained his senses. Hooker, now back on his feet, charged at Murdock for a second time. This time Murdock arm dragged him to the floor, mounted him, and grabbed him around the neck with both hands and pounded the back of his head into the floor.

The police arrived on the scene and started immediately taking people into custody. At this time, four of Murdock's friends were trying to pull him off Hooker. Murdock was in a trancelike state. His right hand was clenched into a tight fist. He's striking Hooker in the head over and over again. The police tried to subdue Murdock but were unsuccessful. Murdock was throwing police officers around effortlessly. One officer pulled a Taser and dry stunned Murdock, but it was ineffective. Another officer deployed his Taser, and when both prongs made contact with Murdock's body, he collapsed to the floor, shaking violently. The rest of the officers pounced on top of Murdock, handcuffing him and hog-tying him up.

Bobby ran over to intervene. "Hey! Hey, boys! Take it easy. The man just got back from the war in Afghanistan. Cut him some slack. This piece of human trash started with us!" All of Bobby's protests were ignored, and the cops dragged Murdock out of the bar and shoved him into the back of a police cruiser to transport him down to the station for booking. Everyone else was detained for questioning.

The officers handling Murdock's booking arrived at the police station. The officers pulled Murdock out of the back of their car and removed the hog-tie restraints. Murdock's demeanor was now calm, but he appeared to still be in a state of confusion, almost unsure as to where he was. He was escorted inside to the inmate receiving area accompanied by two police officers. They approached the counter where Murdock was searched, his pockets were emptied, his picture was taken, and he was fingerprinted. The cops who were present at the scene of the incident informed the intake team of what transpired.

"To be honest, guys, I'd never seen anything like it. It was almost as if he was possessed by a demon," said one cop as he briefed the station sergeant.

"Several guys were sprawled out on the floor, and another was getting his face pounded in," added the supporting arrest officer. Murdock was taken away from the booking area and placed in a holding cell with four other inmates. All but one of them were arrested for battery and other violent crimes. Antonio was one of the four inmates in the cell with Murdock. He was arrested and charged with battery after beating up a family member.

"What they do, tough guy?" Antonio sneered as Murdock just stood there staring through the bars of the jail cell.

"What the hell happened to your face?" jeered another inmate in Murdock's direction. Murdock was leaning against the cell bars, still a bit confused as to what exactly happened and why he was even in jail. The largest inmate in the cell named Tony, standing at approximately 6'3" tall and weighing nearly 245 pounds, made his way toward Murdock. He leaned against the bars about three feet directly beside Murdock. The man noticed Murdock's USMC tattoo on his forearm.

"Well, what do we have here? One of Uncle Sam's little soldier boys in jail." Murdock slowly turned and faced Tony. "Today I'm gonna be ya uncle, punk," Tony said as he reached out to grab Murdock by the shirt. Instinctively, Murdock thrust Tony in the throat with the edge of his hand, crushing Tony's windpipe. Tony fell to the floor like a tree as he began to cough, gagging for air.

The inmate arrested for the lesser crime ran to the bars while literally pissing his pants, shouting, "Help! Help! They're crazy! I want out!"

The station guards came rushing over and entered the cell to find Murdock standing over Tony who was now choking on his own blood. The terrified inmate ran over to the guards but tripped over his own feet and fell face flat. He latched on to one of the officers' legs, sobbing and begging to be placed in another cell.

"Get the hell off me, man," the cop retorted to the inmate.

"Check it out, Jim, he was so happy to see you he pissed his pants." The officers burst out into laughter. The guards rushed Tony to the clinic for treatment, and they relocated Murdock to a solitary confinement cell. Murdock was now sitting alone in silence with no one and nothing but his thoughts to keep him company. The memories of war swirled around the room carried in the distant sounding echoes of explosions, gunfire, and the shrieks of wounded American soldiers. In the opposite corner of the room from where Murdock was sitting, he can see the pale corpse of Will McCormick sitting in the corner leaning against the wall. The head of McCormick turned to Murdock. His eyes opened, and he whispered, "Why did you let me die?"

Murdock stood and started shouting toward the empty corner, "I tried, Will! I tried to save you!"

The guard just outside the cell overheard Murdock shouting. He stepped over to inspect the cell and saw Murdock standing and shouting at the empty corner of the cell. At that time, the front desk radioed the watch guard and informed him of Murdock's military background. The staff sergeant immediately instructed the front desk to contact Murdock's wife.

The watch guard tapped on the cell door as he opened it and said, "Mr. Grey, your wife is here. Let's go."

Murdock exited the cell. He reluctantly glanced at the guard and hung his head low. As Murdock was escorted to the front and made his way around the corner, Nadia caught her first sight of him. She gasped and placed her hand to her face while shaking her head in total disbelief.

"Mickey, what on earth happened to you?" Nadia exclaimed. She teared up as he approached her. She cupped his face between her hands and looked over his condition. "What happened?" Nadia asked in her now-trembling voice.

"I got into a fistfight, and I don't want to talk about it right now," Murdock replied without even looking Nadia in the face.

Murdock walked past her without a hug or any affection and walked ahead toward the exit.

Nadia walked over to the receiving officer and asked, "What happened?" There was a change of shift between the time of Murdock's booking and Nadia's arrival. Therefore, the receiving officer had to research Murdock's profile via the database. "Apparently your husband was involved in a physical altercation with another man. According to eyewitness testimony, the fight broke out over a woman. That's all the info I see from the report, ma'am."

Nadia thanked the officer and struggled to fight back the tears as she made her way toward the exit. *Who could this other woman be? Fighting over her. Really?* Nadia thought to herself. She and Murdock got in their car to go home. Nadia drove silently and in deep thought. She glanced over at Murdock, who was staring blankly out the window.

"So you don't have anything to say for yourself?" Nadia asked angrily. Murdock did not respond. "I prayed every day for you to come back home to me safe. For what? So you could be fighting over another woman!" Nadia exclaimed.

Once the couple arrived home, Nadia made Murdock sleep on the couch until the morning. They went to sleep without saying much else to each other at all.

Chapter 4

The Enemy Within

The next morning, Murdock was standing near the living room entranceway while on the phone with his psychiatrist's office to confirm his appointment. Nadia came downstairs and made her way into the living room with paperwork in her arms, her hair in a messy bun, and her reading glasses sliding down her face.

"Okay, sounds good. I'll see you all then. Thanks," Murdock said as he hung up the phone with the doctor's office. "Sleep okay?" Murdock asked.

"Not really. You?" Nadia replied.

"No," Murdock responded, looking under at Nadia rather sheepish. Nadia wobbled over to the couch to sit down, but she was clearly having a bit of struggle from the weight gain due to her pregnancy. Murdock helped her to take her seat on the couch and slid the coffee table closer to her so she didn't have to strain or stretch.

"Mickey, I'm proud of you for making that call. I know you, and I know how hard it is for you to ask for help," Nadia said while getting comfortable in her seat. "And you should know I trust you, but I have to know what last night was all about." Nadia continued while thumbing through her paperwork.

"I have to go see my counselors to try and figure out what's going on in my head and why. I love you, Nadia," Murdock replied as he sat down next to his wife and gave her a kiss on the forehead.

"I love you too, but you still haven't answered my question." Murdock stood in silence. Nadia was overwhelmed with emotion to the point that she burst into tears. "I'm sorry, I've just missed you so much!"

Murdock turned and faced Nadia. "It's not what it looks like. It was a confusion, a mix-up that just went too far." Murdock sighed and paused. "I missed you too. Both of you," Murdock said as he rubbed Nadia's stomach. "I'm gonna head out to see my counselors. I'll call you when I finish." Murdock made his way out the door. Nadia stood in the doorway, watching him reverse out of the driveway.

Murdock was anxious the entire drive to the psychiatrist's office. *Are they gonna tell me I'm crazy? Can they even help me?* were the thoughts racing through Murdock's mind while on the highway. He now pulled into the plaza where Dr. Feingold's office was located. After he parked, Murdock sat in his car for a moment, his sweaty palms clenching the steering wheel as he attempted to gather control over his emotions and thoughts. Upon entering the office, Murdock made his way over to the front desk counter and greeted the receptionist.

"Good afternoon. Please sign in for me," the young lady instructed Murdock. He took his seat in the waiting room area and grabbed a nearby magazine. Even while he waited to be called, the flashbacks of death and war continued to swirl in his mind. The squeaky hinges of the office door were reminiscent of the doors in that old brick house building where McCormick died.

The office door swung open again. A young female nurse practitioner named Natalie called out, "Murdock Grey!"

Murdock dropped the magazine on the table, stood up, and made his way to the office. Natalie took Mr. Grey's weight, height, and blood pressure. "Come, have a seat in here. Complete this medical history questionnaire, and Dr. Feingold will be with you shortly," Natalie explained.

Dr. Feingold entered Murdock's room. "Good afternoon, Mr. Grey," Dr. Feingold greeted Murdock as he grabbed a chair and sat with Murdock. "First off, I want to thank you for your service to the country," Dr. Feingold said as he opened Murdock's patient folder. Murdock nodded in approval of Feingold's kind gesture. "So my team tells me you've been experiencing high levels of anxiety, hallucinations, and blackout spells. Is that correct?" Feingold asked.

"Yes, all of those things and much worse. I feel like I don't know how to live a normal life anymore," Murdock responded. Dr. Feingold and Murdock spent more than one hour together discussing Murdock's experiences since returning home from Afghanistan.

Murdock walked out of the building slightly distressed in his demeanor. His cell phone rang. "Hey, yeah, look, it's not a good time. Call you back." Murdock hurriedly got off the phone. He got in his car and slammed his hands against the steering wheel several times in frustration. *They can't help me*, Murdock thought to himself as he gazed into his own face in the rearview mirror. His eyes began to fill up with tears. He shook his head, started up his car, and sped out of the parking lot.

Murdock called the local veteran administration's office as he drove.

"Hello, VA's office. How—"

Murdock interrupted the operator. "I'm coming in now. I need help!" As Murdock made his way to the VA's office, the highways began to look like the desert roads of Afghanistan. He started swerving as the visions became more and more vivid. Murdock pulled into the VA hospital parking lot. As he entered the waiting area and made his way to the receptionist, he scanned the room. The lobby was filled with dozens of men and women, all veterans waiting to see the MD. The vast majority of these war heroes were all suffering from symptoms similar to Murdock's. You can see the despair and hopelessness in their faces. Many of them were suffering from anxiety and unable to sleep properly for days. Their faces showed the weariness they all felt inside. The hopes of leading a normal life again seemed like a distant, if not unreachable, reality. One after the other, you can hear the side conversations with other veterans discussing the hellish images of war they can't remove from memory.

"I have to see the MD immediately. Please, I can't wait."

The receptionist motioned her hand toward the lobby and said, "There are a lot of people ahead of you, sir. If you would just sign in and—"

Murdock slammed both his fists on the counter. "Help me now! I need help!" Murdock shouted as two security officers approached the desk.

"Is everything okay here?" the security officer asked. Just as security was about to ask Murdock to take his seat, the doctor came out and said, "It's okay. He can come to the back." Murdock followed Dr. Greene down a long hallway to his office. Murdock placed his hand on the wall, leaning over in a cold sweat. He can hear his own heartbeat racing as he panted for air.

Dr. Greene turned to Murdock and said, "Sir, look at me. Everything is all right now. Follow me." Murdock and Dr. Greene continued down the hall toward his office. They entered the doctor's office.

"Please have a seat," Dr. Greene instructed Murdock as he took his seat behind his desk. "So tell me, what's your name?"

"Murdock Grey," Murdock replied.

"And what brings you to the VA today?"

Once Murdock opened up about his "blackout" episodes, anxiety, and other symptoms, Dr. Greene diagnosed his condition as post-traumatic stress disorder or PTSD. Dr. Greene shared a personal testimony with Murdock of one soldier he recently counseled. The veteran explained to Dr. Greene that he woke up in the middle of the night thinking he had placed an intruding terrorist in a choke hold. Tragically he was actually choking out his wife. Thankfully the wife survived the incident, but you can only imagine the tension this placed on their home and marriage. Dr. Greene explained that one of the fundamental causes behind PTSD is not largely predicated on what these soldiers had seen but rather what they had to do while in war. Dr. Greene went on to explain the horrendous effects that PTSD has had on the veteran community as a whole as well as marriages ending in divorce, children temporarily removed from the home, and other devastating circumstances.

Dr. Greene explained to Murdock the importance of proper treatment and communal and familial support throughout this process. "I was an infantry soldier deployed to Vietnam on two occasions. So trust me when I say, your cooperation in therapy can go a long way."

Murdock agreed to be as cooperative and transparent as possible during his treatment. Dr. Greene provided an antidepression and antianxiety prescription and a continued therapy schedule for Murdock to adhere to.

Murdock exited the VA and called Nadia on his way to the car. "Hey, love, sorry it took so long for me to reach out. I've been at the VA for the past few hours." Nadia asked Murdock to hurry on home because she missed him.

"I have to stop by the store to fill my prescription. Do you need anything?" Murdock asked.

"Eggs, and we need more milk please," Nadia replied.

Murdock parked at the local grocery store, grabbed a hand basket, and headed to the pharmacy. Ralph was the head pharmacist. He knew Murdock and Nadia from the neighborhood. Ralph greeted him, "How's it going, Murdock?"

Murdock nodded his head. "Not too bad, Ralph. Please fill this script for me. I gotta grab a few items."

Ralph agreed. "I'll expedite this for you."

While making his way down the bread aisle, Murdock heard footsteps creeping up behind him. He turned and looked, but no one was there. A chill ran down his spine as he exited the aisle. He opened the door to the milk cooler and grabbed a half gallon of milk. As he closed the door, the reflection of John Brooks flashed behind him.

"John?" Murdock whispered to himself lowly as he turned around. The only person standing there was the stock clerk for the store putting canned goods on the shelf. Murdock lowered his eyes and shook his head in a sense of disbelief. After Murdock grabbed his other groceries, he made his way back to the pharmacy to pick up his prescription.

"The script hasn't been filled just yet. I—"

Murdock slammed his grocery basket on the counter in front of him before Ralph could complete his explanation. "Well, why not!" Murdock demanded.

"Just a few minutes and it will be complete. I apologize for the inconvenience," Ralph responded nervously. Murdock took a deep breath and walked away to place his groceries in the car. Murdock returned to the pharmacy counter. As Ralph handed him his prescription, Murdock looked at him under his brow, his demeanor almost that of someone who was embarrassed, and he apologized to Ralph for his outburst.

"No worries, Murdock, I apologize for any inconvenience. Have a great evening." Murdock got into his car and immediately took one of his antianxiety pills. During his drive home, he began to get drowsy from the medication he took. He was in such a hurry to take his prescription he failed to read all the side effects the drug may cause. Murdock fell asleep at the wheel; his car swerved into the opposite lane of traffic. When the car ran across the median, it jolted Murdock awake. He regained control of the vehicle and pulled over to the side. He took a few minutes to collect his nerves and continued home.

When Nadia saw the headlight turn into the driveway, she hastily got up to meet Murdock at the front door. "My goodness, it's about time you made it home," Nadia said as she embraced her husband. Murdock still appeared a bit drowsy. "Are you okay?"

Murdock paused in a daze. "Yes, I'm fine. Just really tired." Nadia put the groceries away while Murdock went upstairs to take a shower. The two of them were now lying in bed.

Nadia began, "So how was your day at the VA?" Murdock was already beginning to doze off. Nadia nudged him in his side with her elbow. "Hello, we haven't talked all day. Can I at least get five minutes of your time?"

Murdock sat up in bed with his back resting against the headboard. "Sorry, my love. It's this prescription. It makes me tired."

Nadia had a confused look on her face by now. "Prescription? What prescription, Mickey?" Murdock shared the story of what happened at the VA earlier, the discussion he had with Dr.

Greene, and his diagnosis. "Is there a cure for this PTD whatever it's called?" Nadia asked.

"Honestly, I don't know, love. Doc just said as long as I am committed to the treatment plan, chances are my condition can only get better."

Nadia rested her head on Murdock's chest. "Well, just know we are here, and we are not going anywhere." She took Murdock's hand and placed it on her round belly.

"I know, my love, I know," Murdock replied as he pulled her in closely, and the two of them fell asleep.

Chapter 5

True Lies

The next morning, Murdock was up early, showered, and dressed for the gym.

"Honey, I'm heading to the gym. Love you," he said as he leaned over to kiss Nadia on the forehead as she lay in bed.

"Love you too," she mumbled while still half asleep. Around midmorning, Nadia started to stir in bed. She reached across the bed and felt an empty spot. Realizing Murdock wasn't in bed, she tried to keep a balanced perspective and not jump to any wild conclusions, but she also can't help but feel concerned given all the changes she and her husband were going through.

Nadia toasted a bagel and brewed some tea. Just as she grabbed her phone to call her husband, it started ringing. It was her best friend Kathy calling her. "Hey, Ash! What's up?"

Ashley replied, "Hey, girl, I got the day off from work, so if you're free, stop by my house. We need to catch up."

Nadia looked at the empty chair across from her as she contemplated her answer. "What the heck, it's been too long. I'm gonna swing by!" Nadia answered.

*****

Kathy's doorbell rang. She peeked through the window and saw Nadia standing on her front porch. Kathy shrieked in excitement as she opened the door. Both women shouted in joy and excitement as they embraced each other.

"Get in here!" Kathy demanded as she pulled Nadia inside and shut the door behind her. She was in the kitchen prepping dinner for the evening as Nadia stood in the doorway sipping on her tea. After some small talk and playing catchup, Nadia began to open up about all the challenges she and Murdock had been experiencing since he returned from Afghanistan.

"He's not the same. He just seems so distant at times," Nadia explained. Kathy glanced over at Nadia as she grabbed some ingredients out of the refrigerator. "He leaves the house and is gone nearly all day, and I barely get even a text message from him," Nadia continued.

Kathy was now at the counter chopping up veggies and adding ingredients to her beef stew. "Well, don't you start chasing after him either," Kathy retorted.

"And not to mention this other female he was fighting over the week he came home. I'm starting to feel like he might be seeing someone else."

Kathy shook her head and replied, "But you don't know that for sure." Nadia sighed after a sip of her tea and lowered her head. "The only way to be sure before you do something crazy is hire a private investigator," Kathy suggested.

Nadia looked up at Kathy with surprise all over her face. "An investigator… Don't you think that's going too far?"

Kathy placed her knife down on the cutting board, looked at Nadia, and said, "Girl, no! Look, you're pregnant, and you can't worry about whether or not your husband is out here getting into trouble." Nadia took a seat on the barstool across from Kathy as she contemplated her suggestion. "You just want to be sure you know what the whole story is before you make a decision that can affect you and your unborn baby."

Nadia began to nod in agreement with her friend's advice. "Maybe you're right. But where should I start? I don't know any PIs personally."

Kathy smiled as she reached across the counter and patted Nadia on the back of her folded hands. "That's why you're lucky to have a friend like me. I know a place," Kathy replied. With that, Adam, Kathy's husband, came home.

"Hey, love! I'm home!" Adam shouted coming through the door. The ladies exchanged glances at each other and smiled.

"Oh hey, Nadia. I thought that was your car parked out front," Adam said as he entered the kitchen.

"Hey, Adam," Nadia replied.

"Are you and Mickey joining us for dinner?" Adam asked.

"No thanks, maybe next time. I was just heading out, and Mickey should be home by now," Nadia said as she gathered her belongings and walked toward the door.

"How's Mickey doing by the way?" Adam asked.

"He's…he's…," Nadia stammered.

"He's doing better than ever, right, girl?" Kathy quickly interjected.

"Well, tell him I said hey," Adam said.

"Right. Talk to you later, Kat. Take care, Adam." Nadia said her goodbyes and headed to her car.

Nadia pulled into their driveway and noticed Murdock's car. "Mickey?" she called out as she entered the house.

"I'm in here. In the nursery," Murdock replied. Nadia entered the nursery. Murdock was sitting in the rocking chair in the corner thumbing through the photo album Nadia made for him while he was away.

"Hey, love. How was your day?" Nadia asked hesitantly.

"Gym time, therapy at the VA, and some volunteer work while I was there." Nadia shrank back into her own thoughts about her doubts, suspicions, and conversation with Kathy earlier. "Nadia, did you hear me?" Murdock asked.

"I'm sorry…," Nadia replied.

"I said how was your day?" Murdock repeated.

As Nadia looked Murdock in the face, she questioned his intentions. "It was fine. I stopped by Kathy's for a bit. Adam said hey."

The Greys were having dinner in the dining room. The energy between the two of them was distant, cold, and indifferent. Murdock finished his dinner, washed his plate, and put it in the dishwasher. "I'll see you in bed, love. I'm exhausted," Murdock said as he leaned over to kiss his wife on the forehead and made his way upstairs to the bedroom. Nadia was left at the dining room table, alone with nothing but her thoughts and suspicions to keep her company. She sent a text message to Kathy: "Pick you up at your place in the morning."

The next day around midmorning, Nadia showed up at Kathy's house. "I'm outside," Nadia text messaged Kathy.

"On my way out now," Kathy replied via text message. The ladies arrived at the private investigator's office in the city of Sunrise. "Mickey is going to kill me," Nadia whispered to herself, but Kathy overheard it.

"You're not doing anything terribly wrong. You just want to know the truth about what's going on." They got out of the car and walked up toward the entrance of the building. The ladies exchanged a quick glance at each other and entered the building. They approached the front desk security guard.

"We're here for Vinny Parco, Private Investigator," Kathy said. The security officer instructed them to both sign in and have a seat.

"We'll call you when Mr. Parco is available," the security officer said. Approximately fifteen minutes passed when Vinny Parco came to the front.

"Kathy! Long time. You ladies come to my office," Vinny said as he shook Kathy's and Nadia's hands. Nadia and Kathy took their seats in front of Vinny's large cherrywood desk. His office walls were covered by pictures of his friends, his family, his framed college degrees, and his service medals.

"Vinny, thanks for seeing us on such short notice," Kathy expressed. "This is my friend Nadia, and I think she can use your help."

Vinny sat back in his chair now with his arms crossed.

"So where do I start? I mean, I love my husband. I just don't know if I can trust him. He acts so different since returning from Afgh—"

Vinny leaned forward and interrupted Nadia midsentence. "Wait, hold on. You haven't explained to me exactly why you've come here. What's your reasoning?"

"My husband has been very distant lately. He's a good man, but there is something troubling him. Yet he refuses to open up to me about it," Nadia explained.

Vinny started up again. "Look, ma'am, do you need a PI or not?" Vinny asked. "Sounds to me as though you are not entirely sure."

"I…I don't…," Nadia stammered over her words.

Vinny interrupted again. "Okay, if I may suggest, sounds like you want that praying PI Bill Perry Private Eyes." Vinny scoffed. "Sounds like he'll be your guy. I don't want to sound rude, but I don't have time to pray with you for clarity."

"Thanks for shooting straight with us, Vinny. We'll show ourselves out," Kathy said.

Nadia and Kathy exited the elevator on the seventh floor of Bill Perry's Private Eyes office. The ladies by this point felt a bit dejected, and even worse, the waiting area was fairly busy. One of Bill's PIs named Wayne passed by, tipped his fedora, and nodded at the ladies. Wayne may have only one arm, but he had been a faithful agent with the firm for a number of years.

Private Investigator Wayne Weatherford

"Good afternoon, ladies," Wayne said as Kathy and Nadia exited the elevator. The martial artist secretary, Kai, was storming her way down the hall; and by the look on her face, you can tell she was in a terrible mood. Not too far off behind her was a faint tapping noise. Anthony was the blind P.I. with a keen sense almost as if he was being guided from the heavens.

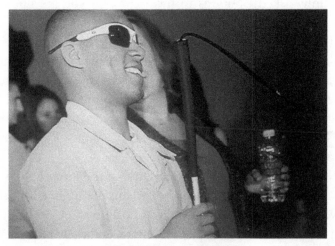

Anthony Alford the Blind P.I.

"Hey, Prophet, where ya headed?" Wayne asked.

"I'll have a consultation appointment with two new clients today," Anthony, the blind PI, replied. Nadia asked for Bill Perry.

Wayne replied, "He's in his office. Is this your first time here?"

Nadia said, "Yes, it is."

Wayne had them sign in at the front. "Follow me," he instructed Kathy and Nadia. An eight-and-a-half-by-eleven stained glass plaque inscribed with the name Bill Perry Private Eyes was mounted on the door leading to Perry's office. Wayne knocked on the door, and Perry motioned his hand for the parties to come in.

Bill Perry was sitting behind his large glass stainless steel desk on a conference call. He motioned for the ladies to sit as he ran through this call with animated high energy. "Yes, yes. You know, I have to call you back. I've got a client walking in now. Okay. Chao." Bill hung up the phone, turned, and extended his hand to Nadia and then to Kathy. "Hi, ladies, welcome to Bill Perry Private Eyes. I'm Bill Perry."

Bill and Kathy shared some small talk. "Kathy, great to see you again. How's Adam?"

Kathy replied, "Great seeing you as well. All is well, Bill, thanks."

"So Vinny sent me a quick text-message brief about your situation, but I'd like to hear it from you." Bill continued, "So, Nadia, you're having troubles with your husband? Can you explain the whole situation?"

Nadia looked over to Kathy, who gave her an encouraging nod. She began, "Well, it started off when he got back from Afghanistan. He's a marine…" Nadia took Bill through a chronology of what had transpired in her and Murdock's life right up to that day.

Bill took a deep breath and exhaled. "I can see how this is troubling you. I'll send a few of my investigators out to see what's going on."

"Mr. Perry, I can't thank you enough for jus hearing me out," said a teary-eyed Nadia.

"Thank me when it's over," Bill replied. He spun to his phone. "Send me Joe, Ron, and the Dream Girls please and thanks."

The Day Dream Girls, Christine, Szu and Kai

Joe, Ron, and the Dream Girls, Danika and Jaiden, all entered Bill's office. Joe and Ron were two dedicated young PIs with up to two years of experience in the industry. Both locals and handsome young men, they can blend in well with nearly any crowd. Danika and Jaiden were nine months into their private investigator intern programs with Perry's firm. These young, street-smart, and very attractive young ladies had been a huge asset to Perry's team across several very diverse assignments during their internship.

"I got a job for you," Bill announced to the group. They all shared a coy glance at each other with a slight grin on their faces in anticipation of what the assignment may entail. Bill gave an overview of the details surrounding Operation Murdock. Each member was given their specific objectives.

"We will begin tailing Murdock tomorrow and see what the day delivers," Bill said and dismissed the group. He shook hands with Nadia and Kathy once more and assured Nadia the firm would do its best to gather the answers she was searching for.

Early the next morning, the PIs took their designated places. While conducting surveillance, Ron was able to collect audio transmissions that helped the team in determining Murdock's itinerary for the remainder of the day. Once Murdock left the house, Joe and Ron began the tail. Joe provided Danika and Jaiden the address of Murdock's afternoon stop. Joe and Ron tailed Murdock into the city and observed him enter the gym. He was presumably inside for approximately one hour and thirty minutes. The PIs observed him exiting the gym, entering his car, and pulling out of the parking lot.

"Ron, be sure to not get too close. We don't want to be spotted," Joe instructed him.

"Not to worry, Nervous Nellie. I got this under control," Ron assured him. Murdock was observed by the team pulling into the VA parking lot and entering the building for his therapy session with Dr. Greene and the staff.

Joe placed a call to Bill to update him on their whereabouts and findings thus far. "Hey, Bill, it's Joe. So far nothing out of the ordinary."

"Good work so far. Keep at it, gentlemen," Bill replied. Surveillance outside the VA lasted for nearly two hours. Joe had his head down jotting some notes in his activity report. Ron nudged Joe on the arm. "Check it out. He's going to the car now."

Joe called Danika, "Hey, Danika, you and Jaiden take your positions. It looks like we are heading your way now." Murdock led Bill's team to a restaurant located on the intercoastal near the city of Lighthouse Point. Murdock left his car with the valet and went inside.

Ron sent a text message to Danika. "He just left valet and is heading inside. Did you make your reservations?"

Danika replied, "Understood. Yes, table is booked."

The hostess approached Murdock. "Welcome to Rachels on the River. Reservation?"

Murdock answered, "Yes. Table for two. Last name Grey."

The hostess replied, "Right this way, sir. Your guest has already been seated." The hostess took him to table number 13. As Murdock approached the table, he can see a brunette with her back toward the entrance.

"Hey, you," Murdock said as he placed his hand on her shoulder.

She turned and smiled at Murdock. "Hello." It's Maria, the young lady from the brawl at the club.

Danika and Jaiden left their luxury rental car to the valet and entered the restaurant. "Too bad they didn't want to meet up on the beach. I could work on my tan," Jaiden said jokingly to Danika.

"Girl, please. You're Colombian. You're naturally tan," Danika jokingly replied.

Jaiden rolled her eyes. "You wouldn't understand."

Danika held up the back of her hand and said, "Well obviously." She continued, "I'm glad we're not on the beach. I burn so bad I look like a big strawberry." The girls laughed together as the hostess greeted them both.

"Hi, ladies, and welcome. Reservations?"

Jaiden responded, "Yes, last name Santos."

The hostess grabbed two menus. "Right this way, ladies." The hostess seated them at table number 12, directly across from Murdock and Maria. Jaiden and Danika ordered drinks while they listened in on Murdock and Maria's conversation. Murdock and Maria ordered lunch and drinks while chatting, mostly small talk.

"Hey, thanks for coming out, Maria," Murdock said as he reached across the table and rubbed Maria on the back of her hand.

Maria looked under at Murdock with a smile. "It's always a treat getting to spend time with you."

Joe sent a text message to Danika. "What's happening?"

Danika replied, "Murdock is having lunch with a brunette by the name of Maria."

Joe leaned over and showed Ron his phone. "Maria? I'd be willing to bet it's the same Maria from that bar fight in our overview notes from Bill."

Ron nodded in agreement. "J, if I were a betting man, I'd put money on your hunch."

Murdock and Maria finished their meals. "Check please." Murdock motioned for the waitress. He paid for the tab in cash, and they made their way to the front toward the valet.

Danika sent a text message to Joe. "They've finished their meal and are heading to the front."

Joe and Ron got in position to capture surveillance and pictures. The PIs observed Murdock calling the valet over and giving him a cash tip. Maria's car was pulled around first. Murdock walked her to the driver's side, pulled her closely to him in a tight embrace, and kissed her on the cheek. Maria got in her car at that point and drove off. Murdock remained at the front of the restaurant awaiting his car. While he waited, he was observed pulling out his cell phone and making a phone call. Using near-field audio devices, the PIs were able to determine he was placing a call to his wife, Nadia.

"Hey, love, how is everything?" Murdock asked.

"I'm fine. At home prepping for dinner."

Murdock got into his car. The remainder of the call's audio was disrupted, but Murdock was observed ending the call as he pulled out of the parking lot.

The PIs continued to tail Murdock in the same fashion for the next several days, collecting audio, picture, and video footage of the couple meeting up at different times of the day and at various locations. Bill called a meeting with Joe and Ron at the end of the week to review their findings thus far.

"Guys, come on in. Grab a seat please," Bill instructed Joe and Ron as they entered his office. "Talk to me. What you got on Murdock so far?" Bill asked. Joe opened the meeting by reviewing his shorthand notes on the couple's routine activities over the past several days.

"We've observed them meeting up at a handful of restaurants, the park, the mall, and hotels," Joe explained. Ron then presented all of the audio, picture, and video footage that corroborated all of Joe's journals concerning Murdock and Maria's activities.

"Good stuff so far, boys. I will update the client," Bill said as he started thumbing through his client file folders.

"We have intel suggesting the couple will be meeting up late this evening near the city of Lighthouse Point," Joe explained.

"Well, don't let me hold ya. Go on and prepare for the evening," Bill replied. After concluding the briefing with Ron and Joe, Bill placed a call to Nadia.

"Hello," Nadia answered.

"Nadia, Bill Perry, how are you?"

Nadia responded, "I'm well, thanks."

"Nadia, let me start by saying I believe in being straightforward and honest with all my clients. Are you okay with that?"

Nadia replied, "Yes."

Bill continued, "Nadia, so far my PIs have observed Murdock meeting up with a young lady by the name of Maria. Does that name sound familiar?"

Nadia paused for a moment in thought. "Actually I remember hearing that name over a phone call between Murdock and his friend Bobby after the bar fight that broke out at his party." Bill continued to review their findings so far and assured Nadia he would keep her in the loop as the investigation progressed. Meanwhile, Ron and Joe had tailed Murdock to Maria's house. Maria was seen opening the door and inviting Murdock to come inside. Video and audio transmissions picked up on the couple chatting inside. After approximately one hour inside the house, Murdock and Maria exited and got inside Murdock's pickup truck and drove off. The PIs tailed them to a small ice cream parlor near Lighthouse Point.

"They have a great butter pecan ice cream here. I know the owners personally," Murdock bragged to Maria. The two of them made an order and sat outside under the umbrellas, engaging in small talk.

"So how is therapy coming along?" Maria asked.

"It's getting easier as time passes," Murdock said as he sort of looked away from Maria.

"Hey, you don't have to be ashamed or anything. We all got problems," Maria said as she made a funny face, leaning into Murdock. Murdock leaned in and kissed the back of her hand as Ron snapped several pictures. After finishing their snack, they dumped the trash, hopped in the car, and continued heading east toward the beaches. Murdock parked and grabbed a large beach towel from the back of his truck. He and Maria strolled over the pedestrian walk and unto the sand. The sun had set, so the PIs had the benefit of night cover and night vision equipment. Murdock and Maria huddled together on the blanket to stay warm from the cool breeze as they stared beyond the lighthouse.

"Ron, are you getting this?" Joe asked.

"Yeah, bud, I got it," Ron replied.

"I know Hooker still has a presence in your life. Why is it so hard for you to keep away from this guy?" Murdock asked.

Maria smirked but with sadness in her eyes and voice. "We've known each other since we were six years old, and we're high school sweethearts," she explained. "He wasn't always like this. I remember him as Toney, before he changed, and I guess that's what keeps part of me on his side." Maria shared a story with Murdock of when she and Hooker were still in high school. It was a Wednesday evening. Maria was following Hooker on her bicycle to the park. She hid her bike in some bushes nearby. Working hard to remain unseen, Maria crept over to where Toney and a suspicious-looking man wearing a hooded jacket were standing. She saw Toney and the man give a quick handshake, exchange some words, and then give another quick handshake before parting ways. All of a sudden, the area was lit up with blue and red flashing lights as local law enforcement moved in on where the two men were standing. The police pulled up and drew their weapons on both men as they shouted instructions.

"Put your hands up! Put 'em up!" shouted one cop.

"Get on the ground now!" yelled another cop. Toney glanced toward the bushes where Maria was hiding. He had no idea she was even there.

The cop shouted again, "Get on the damn ground! Now!" Toney tried to make a run for it.

A cop yelled, "Freeze!" and fired his weapon at Toney who was fleeing the scene. Maria closed her eyes in fear and opened them again to see Toney lying on the ground now bleeding and writhing in pain.

"Ahh, you shot me, man, what the hell! You shot me!" Toney shouted.

"Oh my god! Toney!" Maria cried out as she ran from behind the bushes in the direction of where Toney was lying.

"Maria? What the hell are you doing here?" Toney grunted as the cops subdued him.

"I wanted to know why you were ignoring—" One of the cops grabbed Maria and dragged her away from Toney, tossing her to the ground and placing her in handcuffs.

"Yoo, big man! She ain't have nothing to do with this! Let her go!" Toney protested. Toney was put in the back of an ambulance and taken to the hospital for treatment. Maria was transported down to the station for questioning. Maria sat in the back of the police cruiser anxious and crying the entire ride.

They pulled into the station and parked. The police officer came to her side of the car, opened the door, and instructed her to get out. Maria was placed in an interrogation room for questioning. The room where she was placed had a table, two chairs, and a single bright light. The walls were dark green, one way in, one way out, and a two-way mirror for staff observation on the other side.

Detective Smith walked into the room with a cup of coffee in hand and pulled up a chair. "Are you thirsty or hungry, young lady?" he asked. Maria was silent. "Look, I know you're probably a bit nervous. So I'll make a deal with you." Maria looked under at Detective Smith as she pulled her hair behind her ear. "Answer all my questions to the best of your ability, and we'll get you home as soon as possible. Deal?" Maria sat back in her chair. "Do you know either of the two men involved in tonight's arrest?" Maria nodded. "This one? Or this guy?" Detective Smith said as he pointed to the mug shots of both men. Maria pointed to Toney's photo. "Do you know the purpose behind their meeting?"

Maria said, "No."

Detective Smith sipped his coffee again. "And did Toney know you were present?" Maria shook her head no. Detective Smith made a notation. "Did you know your boyfriend was a drug dealer?" Maria sat silent staring at the table. "Why were you there?" Detective Smith continued to question her.

"I just wanted to know why my boyfriend was ignoring me, okay. Where is Toney? Can I please go now?" Maria replied.

"Okay, Maria, I have no further questions at this time. If we need you, we know how to find you," Detective Smith said with a smirk on his face as he stood up and exited the room. Maria retrieved her personal belongings from the front and asked if she could be taken to the hospital where Toney was transported.

A cop heading to the hospital replied, "You can ride with me."

Toney was sitting up in bed, handcuffed to the rail while watching television when Maria walked into his room. Toney glared at her, furious and agitated. "You're so stupid! Why the hell were you there, Maria?" Toney asked.

"I already told you," Maria replied.

"What did ya tell the cops then?" Toney scoffed.

"Nothing, I didn't tell them anything," Maria rebutted, her voice now trembling. "They told me you were dealing drugs to that man. Is it true?" Toney turned his head away from Maria. "Is it true, Toney?" Maria repeated the question.

"Yeah, it's true. So what now? Ya gonna leave me?"

"No, I love you," Maria answered.

"You're going to regret this, Maria."

Maria shook her head and said, "It's my decision to make. You can't push me out."

Toney pushed himself up in the bed to sit up straight. "I don't want you to leave, but you gotta decide, Maria," Toney said as he winced in pain.

"I'm here to stay," Maria said as she sat on the side of the bed, leaned over, and kissed Toney.

Danika and Jaiden were nearby with friends on the beach where Murdock and Maria were seating. They appeared to be enjoying the company of their friends, but they were both eavesdropping on the conversation between Murdock and Maria.

"Really?" Jaiden said to Danika.

"Bleeding heart." Danika scoffed as she rolled her eyes.

Murdock and Maria packed up and exited the beach. Ron and Joe followed the couple back to Maria's, where Murdock dropped her off. As Murdock pulled into his driveway, he noticed Bobby's car parked in the front. He walked inside and hung his keys on the hook by the door. He heard Bobby's and Nadia's voices coming from the living room area.

"Hey, Bobby. You come to steal my wife?" Murdock jokingly said.

"I'm not stealing anyone," Bobby responded sternly.

Murdock took a second look at Bobby. "You all right?" he asked. Nadia was visibly upset from crying. "Did something happen to Janine?"

"Janine is fine. Can uh...can we talk? Outside, bro?" Bobby asked hesitantly.

"What about? And why can't we just talk in here?" Murdock said, sounding slightly annoyed.

"Just grab a beer and meet me on the patio, man," Bobby retorted. Murdock followed Bobby to the patio and pulled up a chair.

"Yes." Murdock appeared visibly agitated at this point.

"What's going on with you, man?" Bobby asked.

"What do you mean? Spit it out, man," Murdock scolded him.

"Mickey, I'm your friend, you know that. We can tell each other anything," Bobby replied. Murdock nodded his head in agreement.

"Explain to me why I just spent the last three hours being a shoulder for your wife to cry on. Your pregnant wife, Mick," Bobby scolded him.

"You watch your tone, Bob. What exactly are you trying to get at?" Murdock fired back.

"Look, I know it's difficult getting back to a normal way of life after what you've been through but—"

Murdock interjected, "Normal? What'd ya mean by normal, Robert?"

"Whatever happened over there, whoever you were there. It's not the same here."

Murdock stood up out of his chair and walked to the edge of the patio. "You've got to be kidding me." Murdock scoffed as he took a swig of his beer.

"Your wife is—"

Murdock cut him off. "Who do you think I was over there?"

Bobby shook his head in disagreement with what Murdock was saying. "That's not what I'm saying, man. I—"

Murdock cut him off again. "Do you remember Will at all? Huh?" Murdock elevated his voice.

Bobby stood up. "Yes, I do."

Murdock's voice slightly cracked. "He's dead, Bobby! Dead! Never coming back!" Bobby hung his head low. "I held him in my arms as he died! I have to live with that! Every single day!" Murdock shouted. Bobby was silent. "You don't know what it's like to watch a man die! You don't know what it's like to have blood on your hands!" Murdock continued his rant. "You don't know what it's like to have to kill a man. So don't come into my damn house and judge me! Criticize me!" Murdock turned and walked back into the house where Nadia was sitting. Nadia was on the couch, clenching a pillow. Her eyes were bloodshot from all the crying she'd been doing.

Murdock walked up to her and embraced her. "I'm sorry. I'm so sorry." He kissed her on the forehead, grabbed his keys, and left.

Chapter 6

New Beginnings

Two days had passed. Murdock did not return home but instead spent a few days at his buddy Fred's house. Bill's team of PIs continued their surveillance of Murdock and Maria.

"Honestly, I don't know what to make of this Murdock case," Danika said to Jaiden as she pulled her hair back.

"I feel the same way, girl. They're not doing anything," Jaiden replied.

"Yeah, besides talking. She's clearly into him." Danika continued her rant.

"Oh yeah, how can he not notice? She's always two seconds away from jumping on him, and he's just sitting there all serious but gentleman-like," Jaiden added to the rant.

"Women go for the serious but gentleman types nowadays. It's refreshing from the widespread epidemic of arrogance," Danika continued.

Meanwhile, Murdock and Maria's conversation in her car continued. "I'm gonna go to the courthouse and request a restraining order against Hooker. I was talking to my cousin Linda about it the other night," Maria said to Murdock.

"I think that would be a wise thing to do, Maria," Murdock said as he sighed and laid his head against the headrest. "He shouldn't have the privilege to be near you."

Maria looked at Murdock, smiled, and nodded in agreement. Her phone rang. The screen showed "Tio Max." She answered the phone. "Hola. Tio Max, como estas?"

"My Maria, I have heard that you are going to get a restraining order on Toney."

Maria's trembling voice responded, "Yes, Tio. I am. I know you like him, but he's changed so much. You can't see it because you're not here."

Uncle Max responded, "Men are like sheep. You've got to learn how to herd them. He loves you. Promise me you will work it out with him. You won't find another man like him." Maria shook her head in disbelief at what she was hearing. Murdock sat in silence listening to the exchange. Maria scolded her uncle.

"That's exactly what I am hoping for, Tio!" Maria shouted. "You don't understand what's been going on. It hurts me that you are taking his side on this. He's a bad person!" Maria continued scolding her uncle.

"Hmm. Aren't we all though?" Uncle Max scoffed in his reply.

"I can't do this right now. I'm driving. I have to go, Tio." Maria glanced over in Murdock's direction as she proceeded to hang up the phone. Tears were beginning to well up in her eyes. Murdock asked if she was okay. In that moment, she took a quick look into her rearview mirror and saw a recognizable car following her. "Oh no!" Maria exclaimed.

"What? What is it?" Murdock asked.

"Speak of the devil and he will appear. Hooker is following us!" Maria said. She accelerated her car. "Hang on!" she instructed Murdock as she raced speeds down the road. Maria was swerving in and out of traffic and nearly struck a pedestrian as she pulled up to a crosswalk. Hooker was in a car filled with his toughest men. They were in high pursuit of Maria's car.

Meanwhile, the Dream Girls were also in pursuit as Hooker chased Murdock and Maria. "What the hell are they doing?" Danika asked.

"Now we've got some action," Jaiden replied as she held on to the armrest with a grin on her face.

"Call Bill now, please," Danika instructed Jaiden.

"I'm already on it, girl," Jaiden responded.

Meanwhile, Maria was nearly having a nervous breakdown through all of this. "Why is he like this? He's the one who left me! I didn't leave him. He just can't stand the fact that I can be happy without him," Maria ranted. "He just wants me to be unhappy without him!" Maria continued her rant. She was approaching a nearby shopping center on the corner.

"Turn off in here," Murdock instructed her as he pointed toward the shopping center. Maria saw her opportunity and took a hard right turn into the shopping center. "Okay, I think we lost him. Let's go sit inside this restaurant until things cool off," Maria said. The adrenaline rush from the car ride had slightly disturbed Murdock's PTSD. He began to hear the echoes of McCormick's voice being carried across the parking lot. He paused in his steps as he and Maria walked toward the restaurant. He looked back to the parking lot, but no one was there.

"Hey, what's the matter? You okay?" Maria asked in a puzzled manner.

"Looks like I have to enter the place of hell again. Seems like I can't escape it! But today I will…," Murdock replied as he gazed into the empty parking lot.

"No, no. Let's just get inside please," Maria said as she tugged Murdock's arm. Hooker and his men spotted Maria's car in the parking lot of the plaza.

"There it is, Hook! That's her car right there," said one of Hooker's men. Hooker and his people pulled up in the parking lot with screeching tires.

"Yo, Hook, you know we're in Sutol's territory," said Hooker's cousin Max.

"I don't give a crap. There is something in this place that belongs to me, and I'm not leaving until I get it!" Hooker scolded his cousin. Sutol was the head of a rival gang to Hooker, and both men's organizations had been fighting for control of the Fort Lauderdale market for years.

"Can I help you folks with—" The hostess was interrupted by Murdock and Maria's mad rush into the diner. They brushed into her.

"Yes, please, a table for two. Can we just sit here?" Murdock quickly insisted.

"Yeah sure, here are some menus. Your waiter will be out momentarily," the hostess explained as she sat the couple.

"I think we lost them," Maria said.

Murdock let out a disgruntled sigh. "It's not about that," Murdock said in an annoyed manner.

"What's the matter?" Maria asked in concern as she reached out to rub the back of his hand.

Murdock paused. "Nothing. I-I'm just…" Murdock paused again in midsentence.

"It's okay. You can tell me," Maria said encouragingly.

"It's Nadia. She's been really depressed lately. I think it may have something to do with me being out so much."

Maria sat back in her chair. "Does she know you're out with me?" she asked hesitantly. She began a conversation with herself in her own mind. *Wow, haven't even thought once about this man's wife. Messing up big time. What are you doing?* All of these thoughts were racing through Maria's head as she sat at the table with Murdock.

"No, no, she wouldn't understand," Murdock replied.

Maria patted Murdock on the back of his hand, while she actually was struggling with her own internal feelings of guilt and remorse. "Maybe she'll be fine. Try not to worry," Maria suggested. Bill's team of PIs entered the restaurant and took their places near Murdock and Maria's table.

Meanwhile, as fate would have it, Sutol and his men were finishing up a big drug transaction across the street from where Hooker and his men had pulled in. Caesar, one of Sutol's men, pointed out Hooker and his men across the street.

"What the hell are they doing on our turf?" Sutol asked angrily. Sutol and his men pulled up on Hooker and his men and hopped out of their cars, staring down Hooker and his people. "Who told you that you could step foot in my city?" Sutol asked Hooker.

"I called ya mother last night and asked for permission, punk." Hooker scoffed. Max, Hooker's cousin, spit on Caesar's shoes; and instantly a fistfight broke out. Everyone inside the restaurant can hear and see what was transpiring in front of the restaurant. People started dropping their silverware and gathering their belongings to exit the diner.

"I think it's time for us to get going," said one man to his wife and kids.

The scuffle between Caesar and Max advanced toward the front window of the diner. Another man from Sutol's camp charged at Max and Caesar, tackling both men, breaking through the front window of the diner. The men landed right across the table of the family that was sitting and having lunch. Pandemonium had erupted in the diner. Staff and customers were running left, right, back, and forth. The manager was doing his best to restore order. Sutol's and Hooker's men continued to fight outside.

Back inside the diner, a mother and her kids made a dash for the back exit; but in the midst of all the chaos, one of her children who happened to be crippled was separated from her. Now dazed and confused, this little five-year-old boy was in serious trouble. His mother turned and noticed he's gone. She spotted him across the room. "Cameron! Cameron, don't move, baby. I'm coming!" She attempted to crawl from underneath the table, but someone pulled her back.

Caren, mother of crippled child

"Lady, don't go out there. You'll get yourself killed!" said the man.

"Cameron! Come here, honey, come to Mom! You can do it!" shouted the boy's mother. By this time, there were scores of people in this restaurant. Languages from different continents were in the air (Russian, German, French, and so on). One of Sutol's men outside the restaurant pulled his firearm, took aim at Max inside the restaurant, and fired a round at him. Danika saw the man when he was taking aim at Max and realized that the young boy Cameron was in the cross fire. She ran from under the table and leaped in front of Cameron, pulling him to the floor. As she landed, the bullet grazed her on the arm.

"Danika!" Joe shouted across the room.

"I'm okay!" Danika shouted back at Joe. "The bullet grazed me."

The mother was even more hysterical. "No! No! My baby! Is he okay?"

"Yes! He's okay. I got him. Stay where you are, ma'am," Danika responded. Police sirens swarmed the area as cops flooded the parking lot, hopping out of their cruisers with guns drawn. Several of Hooker's and Sutol's men made a run for it. Sutol hopped on a motorcycle and peeled out of the lot in the opposite direction from the police. A cruiser peeled out in high-speed pursuit of Sutol. Hooker, Caesar, and Max were all held at gunpoint and handcuffed by law enforcement. Slowly order was returned to the diner.

"Murdock, are you okay?" Maria asked.

"Yes, I'm fine. You?" Murdock replied. Hooker tried to stand and shout something at Maria, but the cops forced him into the back of the squad car and took him to jail.

Murdock turned to Maria.

"Just worried about you," Maria said as she held on to Murdock's arm. "I could love you. I could be selfish and tell you that I love you and ask for you to stay with me," Maria continued.

Murdock stared at her as he raised his eyebrows, looking surprised. He pulled Maria in close to hug her and placed a kiss on her forehead. "Is this your way of saying goodbye?" Murdock asked.

"Yes," Maria responded.

"I want you to take care of yourself. I will always be here for you, if you ever need anything at all," Murdock said as he looked at Maria in an assuring manner.

Meanwhile, the police continued questioning witnesses, and EMTs were tending to a few people who were injured during the incident, including Danika. Bill Perry had placed a call to Nadia earlier on during the high-speed chase and informed her of the whereabouts of the PIs and Murdock. As Murdock and Maria were saying their goodbyes, Nadia whipped into the parking lot, got out of her car, and walked up to the caution-tape area.

"Mickey! Mickey!" Nadia shouted as she waved her arms in the air, attempting to get Murdock's attention. Maria happened to be walking in the direction of where Nadia was standing. Maria sized her up from her puffy, teary eyes to her swollen pregnant belly. Maria looked down and sighed. The feelings of guilt began to conjure up inside of her mind again.

"Hey," Maria said softly with her now-hoarse voice.

"Yes?" Nadia said, looking rather puzzled. Maria lifted the caution tape and beckoned for Nadia to come through.

"Ma'am, who are you? And where are you going?" the nearby officer asked.

"It's my husband. My husband is here. Please I—"

The officer interrupted, "Come on through, ma'am." The cop was remorseful seeing she was pregnant. Maria led Nadia to the back of the ambulance where Murdock was being checked out by EMTs and questioned by the police. Nadia approached Murdock. With frustration in her heart, she can't help but ask, "What happened this time?" A look of disappointment was all over her face.

Murdock stammered over his words nervously because he didn't really know how much Nadia knew. "Look…honey. It's a long story, but I can explain," Murdock said.

"Oh, it's a long story. It's always a long damn story with you, Mickey!" Nadia scolded him. She broke down and started to cry. "Do you know how much it hurts me to see you like this? And to lie to my face!" Nadia ranted. "I'm carrying your child in me! How could you disrespect me like this!" Nadia continued her rant.

Murdock looked at her with shame across his face. "Nadia, I'm sorry… Look—"

Nadia interrupted him. "Answer me this: have you been going out with another woman?"

Murdock nearly turned pale in the face. He took a hard swallow. "Yes, but not what you think…" Murdock's statement sent Nadia over the edge. A heartbreaking scream came bellowing out of Nadia. She turned and ran away from him. Nadia ducked under the caution tape and headed toward her car. Crying hysterically, she leaned against the trunk to try to collect herself. All the thoughts of insecurity, doubt, and anger consumed her mind.

He cheated on you. You're nothing to him. No one really likes you. He only cares about the baby, Nadia's thoughts continued. Almost in a trancelike state, Nadia was drowning in her own thoughts. She inadvertently stepped out in front of an oncoming car. The driver slammed on the breaks, bringing the car to a screeching halt about one foot away from Nadia. Startled by this, Nadia collapsed in the street. She was still semiconscious, though the world appeared fuzzy. She can feel her stomach begin to tighten, but she was unable to move at the moment.

Murdock witnessed what had happened and lost all composure. He tried to leave the scene of the incident at the diner, but the police won't let him. "That's my wife over there! Get outta my way!" Murdock shouted.

"Sir, calm down. We can't allow you to go over there. The EMTs will handle it," the police commanded as they restrained Murdock. Two pastors from a local church happened to be passing by the area. Both men hopped out of their car along with the driver and ran over to offer help to Nadia. The men helped the EMTs get Nadia on the gurney, and they slipped her an invitation to the church. Nadia grabbed the card and held on to it, but she was almost fully deranged at this point. Her emotions were on an entirely different level. She was screaming and shouting, "Let me die! Let me die! I can't live like this any longer!"

The EMTs had to administer some sedatives to relax her during the ride to the emergency room. Nadia's best friend Kathy happened to be a nurse at the hospital. Ironically Kathy was pulling into the back at the same time as the ambulance that was transporting Nadia. The EMTs placed Nadia on a stretcher and wheeled her into the hospital. Meanwhile, Kathy was collecting her lunch bag and other items on the passenger side of her car; she just so happened to leave her driver's side door unlocked.

Back inside, the nurses tending to Nadia unbuckled her from the stretcher and were going to have her lie in one of the beds, but Nadia was still in a state of emotional derangement. She pulled away from the nurses and ran out the door, nurses and staff running behind her. As Nadia made her dash out the door, she recognized Kathy' car. Nadia swiftly opened her driver's side door as Kathy was gathering her items on the passenger side. She sat in the driver's seat still crying and emotional.

"Nadia?" Kathy exclaimed. "What are you doing here?" Kathy was puzzled. Nadia did not respond to Kathy and instead proceeded to start her car and reverse. Kathy had no choice but to jump in the passenger seat. "Look, I don't know what's going on, but please pull over so I can drive," Kathy suggested.

Nadia pulled to the side of the road, and the ladies swapped positions. "Just drive please," Nadia said. Kathy drove down the highway. "I love my husband so much, but he came back home to be with another woman! I just can't take it!" Nadia shouted as she combed her hands through her hair and dropped her hands to her sides. As she did this, she felt the card in her left pocket she grabbed from the pastor at the Abundant Life Church. "Take me here please," Nadia said to Kathy as she showed her the church card.

As they pulled up to the church, Nadia exited the vehicle before it came to a complete stop. She entered the sanctuary while service was still ongoing. She looked around at the congregation, noticing everyone seemed so peaceful. She longed for this same peace here and now. The minister was preaching on the story of Lazarus and his resurrection from the dead by Jesus of Nazareth. Nadia walked down to the altar as fast as she could while the minister was still preaching and cried out, "Help me! Please, GOD, help me!" Nadia interrupted the sermon.

The congregation stared on in surprise and disbelief at what just happened. "Church, here we have a child of GOD surrendering her will at the altar. Don't just stare. Extend your hands toward her, and help me pray for her peace," the pastor said to the church.

*****

Back at the diner incident, Murdock was completing his statement and interview with law enforcement concerning what transpired. "Am I free to go now?" Murdock asked.

"Uh yeah, looks like we got everything we need from you. You may have to appear in court depending on how this all plays out," the cop replied. Murdock sprinted toward the corner of the plaza and ordered a taxicab back to where his truck was parked. He jumped in his pickup and peeled out, heading in the direction of the hospital where Nadia should've been transported. Murdock was speeding down the highway as he exited the interstate. He pulled up to the hospital, went to the front desk, and gave a description of his wife to intake nurses.

"Sir, that woman literally ran out of our custody a little over an hour ago," the nurse replied.

"Well, where did she go?" Murdock asked with desperation in his voice.

"She jumped in the car of one of our nurses and peeled out of here. We tried to stop her," the nurse explained.

Kathy, it must be Kathy, Murdock thought to himself. He left the hospital and hopped on the highway heading to Kathy's house. Murdock was speeding down the interstate and exited the highway. As he made his way down a main road, he glanced to his right while at a stop light and recognized a familiar bumper sticker on a familiar vehicle. Murdock snapped his fingers and said, "Yeah, that's Kathy's car. They might be in there." Murdock was distraught. "GOD, please don't let my wife leave me. I need help," Murdock prayed silently to himself. Curious enough, he decided to make a U-turn and head back toward the church.

Murdock sped up after the U-turn he made. Suddenly he saw a flash of bright white light, and something passed his window, and then something else. Could it be an angel? Murdock looked up and saw angels were covering the sky, and he screamed out and ran off the road. Cars were running off the shoulders of the road. People were falling out of their vehicles, crying out, and praying at the sight of angels filling the sky. The presence Murdock felt can be likened to a light, the purest light anyone had ever seen.

"GOD, what is this?" Murdock asked in fear and awe. Not knowing what else to do, he bowed his head and prayed, "Lord GOD, I open my heart, and I invite you inside. Forgive me of my sins. I surrender to you here and now. Help me, GOD, help me." Tears filled up Murdock's eyes. It was as though the presence of this light saturated the earth and permeated through all those who inhabited the land. A moment in time, the will of GOD done on earth as it is in heaven. You could search high and low, but not an ounce of greed could be found among men. The orphan and the widow were taken care of, the homeless had refuge, and the poor were blessed beyond measure. A moment in time, the earth and the skies were cleansed from pollution and smog. Men were kind to their neighbor and cared for their animals. Children were allowed to live and let live free from the threat of natural disasters or calamities.

Cars were running off the road. People were looking up all over the place, getting out of their cars, bowing, and praying; some were making signs of the cross. The sky was filled with angelic figures, and some appeared ready to do battle. The look on their faces told the tale of centuries of anticipation: the King of kings JESUS was drawing near.

The news channels were covered with headlines across the country. Unnatural phenomenon was what the headlines read. The weather was altered. There were thunder and lightning, and the wind was howling through the streets. People were frantically running in every direction. The meteorologist had no words to describe what they were witnessing.

"The radars are going off the charts!" meteorologist Erik Salna said on air. Back at the front desk reporting station, both anchors simply had a blank stare on their face.

"I'm speechless," said one anchor as the news went off the air.

Murdock finished his prayer, gathered himself, and made his way to the church. The power of the pure light was all around the church. Murdock was filled with fear, but not a fear of harm, but rather a fear of reverence and respect. As Murdock ran toward the church, the archangel Michael sat at the peak of the church just above the entrance, gazing down at him. Murdock was scared. He covered part of his head, bent down and forward, and ran through the entrance as fast as he could. The pastor's sermon was interrupted again, this time by Murdock entering the sanctuary.

"Come in, my child. You are welcomed here," the pastor said to Murdock as he beckoned for him to come inside.

"I'm sorry, but my wife needs to know I love her." Murdock began his speech. He was now looking directly at his wife, who's sitting down by the altar. "I love you. I may not show it sometimes, but I do. I may not act it sometimes, but I do. I need help. I need you." Murdock pleaded with his wife.

Nadia stood, gazing into her husband's eyes. She could see a change; his gaze had been made new. "I forgive you. Just come home to us," Nadia said tearfully as she smiled, looked down, and rubbed her belly. Murdock and Nadia came together and embraced each other in a tearful reunion at the altar. The congregation embraced Murdock and Nadia into the fold as they took their places. The pastor now continued his message on Lazarus being raised from the dead. The sanctuary was filled up with fog as the sound of wings making a flapping noise filled the church and the sanctuary. A sense of anticipation fell upon the congregation.

Day Dream Angels

The hearers of the word realized that war is not the end, mental illness is not the end, and death is not the end. A man of war like Murdock found comfort in the truth that the death of his fallen comrades was not in vain, nor did it mean the end of what they could be. Their legacy lives on through the lives of the people who refuse to forget them. The wives of dead soldiers discovered comfort in the truth of the resurrection, knowing that one day a body and a new life will be gifted to their husbands and wives who died in honor of service. Suddenly the sanctuary was filled with angels standing. They could be clearly seen in the midst of the congregation.

The congregation began screaming, fainting, and running in fear. It was total pandemonium, and some were shouting and praising GOD. The shouting of the saints was drowned out by a massive earthquake. A flash of lightning struck at the center of the fog near the altar, and JESUS appeared. The screams could not have gone any higher, but at seeing the King of kings, the screams were deafening, and the floor was covered with people fainting and screaming prayers out loud as they looked with disbelief that JESUS was there among them. The light that was coming from JESUS made it hard to stare at him. He stood in silence, and peace fell upon the church. He only looked at the congregation briefly. There was a tomb erected in the sanctuary for a sermon such as this. JESUS raised his arm toward the tomb and commanded, "Lazarus, come out!" Suddenly Lazarus emerged from the tomb wrapped in his burial garb, and the congregation started screaming again because JESUS showed them his power was beyond anybody but him JESUS, the King of kings.

All of a sudden, American soldiers from all branches of the military followed out in full uniform, and with their stare, you just knew JESUS is Lord! Sarah Brooks, the wife of John Brooks, recognized him with strength just seemingly flowing from him, standing at the altar in his new alive body. Sarah was screaming and jumping in disbelief. Her kids started crying and screaming, "Daddy, Daddy!" The families of fallen soldiers were screaming and some fainting at the sight of seeing their families back from the dead. They knew this could only be from GOD LORD JESUS. Nobody else could do this but him. Another loud clap of thunder and lightning knocked the roof of the church as the heavens opened up. The voice of GOD spoke, "The devil came to steal your body, but I came to save your soul!"

The congregation dispersed and ran outside looking toward the heavens as JESUS disappeared into the clouds. Fighter jets flew overhead with a sound of thunder. They looked ready to unleash firepower on the enemy and military branches of all types outside that would put fear in any enemy's eyes. Snipers, SWAT, and the police surrounded the church. Even battleships were mobilized in the harbor. Guns were ready for battle.

"The enemy came to kill, steal, and destroy, but I have come that you might have life and have it more abundantly," the pastor quoted a verse by JESUS of Nazareth in the Bible. Murdock lifted his eyes above the altar, facing the light and turning his back upon the shadows of his past, and said, "We went through hell, but we've arrived at heaven's gate." With everything going on, Murdock heard a sound that occasionally came up in his head just blaring ("I want to be an American soldier" by ABSOLOOT). His stare faded, knowing that he was free from PTSD.

A special Thanks to Bobby White for your support on this project. We Salute you Sir for the tireless hours through the VFW POST 8195 that you put in helping our Veterans who are dealing with Post Traumatic Stress Disorder. The before mentioned Man Marty is proof that the work that you do for our Veterans WORK. I quote (THAT MAN SAVED MY LIFE) I heard it from multiple Veterans & you deserve recognition for that. Thanks again for inviting myself & Wayne to Post 8195 to get the unbelievable stories straight from the Veterans who were there on the front lines to give us, The American People the Freedom we enjoy today. You Sir & all Veterans are truly the Heroes of America. God bless you & we pray for your continued service.

Getting the Word Out

About the Author

I wasn't supposed to be born. My mother and father, Mr. and Mrs. Percy and Irene Perry, had to make a decision not to abort me. My mom's life was at risk, and she had to gamble her own life to save mine; you see, I had to be born. I had to deliver this book slated for a movie. My mom gambled, and thank GOD I'm still here. My childhood was great. I grew up in the South, in a small town named Spring Hope in North Carolina. The environment there was like the *Little House on the Prairie, Happy Days*, and *Cheers* (where everybody knew my name) all rolled into one. During my teen years, I moved to New York in a place called Fort Apache, the Bronx. There I began my private investigation education just being on the streets. My neighborhood was ruled by the Savage Skulls Gang; eventually I became friends with them, and they became my guardian angels. The mean streets of New York by way of Fort Apache, the south Bronx, 125th Street in Harlem, and the Marcy Projects in Brooklyn became my school ground; the streets educated me.

I soon started skip tracing for Citibank where I handled all kinds of banking cases. I then got involved in the kidnapping case involving the Flower Children and a case that made *New York News* bulletin as a professional hit that kept me hiding in plain sight for several months. Everything happens for a reason, and all of these situations led me to Vinny Parco, a private investigator most commonly known for his show on Court TV. There I got a college education in the private education industry. I worked at Viacom a short time and even worked undercover private investigation at Central Park and for events like "Save the Rainforest" on MTV. I later moved to South

Florida with my wife Dorla and opened my own private investigation agency and began working on cases that ranged from cheating spouses to hired hit men, murder, missing persons, veterans with post-traumatic stress disorder, and human trafficking. My life prepared me for this book, but GOD gave me this book. This story took two years plus to write, and it seemed to only come to me in church. Looking back now, it really came together like a jigsaw puzzle.

We are real private investigators. This is real life, and sometimes the dangers involved outweigh the benefits.

This is me.

CPSIA information can be obtained
at www.ICGtesting.com
Printed in the USA
BVHW071235110621
609348BV00004B/635

9 781098 063450